A

CANDLELIGHT REGENCY SPECIAL

Very Sad these poor boys
All the villans (quite a few)
get theirs. A comedy of
errors. But basicly when
boy ment girl they fell in
Love A Fist Sight,

THE AVENGING MAID

Janis Susan May

A CANDLELIGHT REGENCY SPECIAL

Published by
Dell Publishing Co., Inc.
1 Dag Hammarskjold Plaza
New York, New York 10017

ISBN: 0-440-10329-0

Printed in the United States of America
First printing—December 1980

To my parents,

Aletha and Donald May,
all my love

THE
AVENGING
MAID

CHAPTER ONE

Beatrice, Lady Mickleham, smiled complacently and nodded, setting the ostrich plumes which crowned her turban to swaying dangerously. Her ladyship felt quite proud of herself and rightfully so; even for such an early party it was quite a respectable, even stellar turnout. The ballroom at Mickleham House was large and filled with the cream of the ton. The young girls were as beautiful as butterflies, whirling about the room in their whites and pastels, and the men almost equally divided between rich evening dress and the more dashing and colorful military uniforms which were the sole reminder that war raged on two fronts in this year of 1812.

Let the other hostesses complain that London was thin of company at this time of year, that the season was too young for anyone important to be in town; Beatrice Mickleham needed no such excuses, for her parties were famous throughout the ton and invitations were almost as highly prized as Almack's vouchers.

"Such a lovely gathering, my dear. You've done it again," murmured Mrs. Stanhope-Fredericks, languidly fanning herself.

Lady Mickleham looked at her sister with affection. Despite their years, it was easy to see how the two Barrett sisters had captured the Town, both making brilliant matches in their first Season. Beatrice, the older and more striking of the two, had taken the eye of Lord George Mickleham, leader in political circles, dandy of the first stare, and confirmed bachelor, twice her age. No one had been more surprised than he when one of the accredited beauties of the Season had accepted his offer, but no marriage had ever been more happy. Beatrice bore him a son, made an admirable hostess, and now, more than eight years after his passing, declined to remarry, even affecting half-mourning when the mood overtook her.

Arabella, the younger and more delicate sister, had also surprised Society by accepting Mr. Augustus Stanhope-Fredericks. It had been the talk of the ton for quite two weeks when Augustus offered for Arabella Barrett and was accepted. A bluff, straight-talking outdoors sort of man, Augustus was happiest when riding the estate with his bailiff or taking a fence at breakneck speed during the hunt. Arabella Barrett was a frail woman whom two consecutive dances exhausted. Still, despite such differences, the union had been happier than most. After three years and two miscarriages, Arabella produced a daughter, Phillipa, and some ten years later, after much difficulty, a son, Arnold.

"What a pity that Lord Ronald can't be here tonight."

"Yes. He would so have enjoyed it," Beatrice said. Indeed, Lord Ronald was such a nice boy, so well behaved and such an asset to any gathering, as it behooved any boy of hers to be. Still, he was needed more abroad than at home, especially since the Corsican monster seemed intent on gobbling up all of Europe.

"So kind of you to do such a ball for Phillipa. After such a start to the Season as this, I fear the other hostesses will be hard put to match it."

Lady Mickleham smiled dryly. "Precisely my intention. Besides, it is the least I could do for my only niece. This is her second Season, after all," she said kindly, knowing what a tender spot it was with her sister that Phillipa had refused six—six!—perfectly respectable offers, including one from a duke, though she could hardly blame her niece or any gently bred young female for turning down old Lowood, who was fifty if he was a day and had none too savory a reputation.

"Where is Phillipa?"

Arabella delicately pointed with her fan. "There. The last couch. She is having some lemonade."

"Who's that with her? Faith, it's Longstreet!"

"I believe it is. He is most attentive to her."

"Longstreet . . . fine family, fair fortune. He's Arkwright's heir, isn't he?" Beatrice's mind began to work feverishly. *Heir to an earldom and a good-looking man in the bargain. . . . What a catch if Phillipa can pull it off. It will take some delicate handling, though . . .*

The objects of this plotting, quite unaware of the scrutiny to which they were being subjected, sat most companionably a little way from the dance floor, deep in a discussion of horses and hunting. Had Phillipa's mother and aunt been privy to the thoughts coursing

13

through Sir Rupert Longstreet's somewhat thick head, they would have been extremely gratified, for he found Miss Phillipa Stanhope-Fredericks to be a fine sort of girl, level-headed and no doubt a prime goer on the hunting field. She could actually talk to a man, and didn't make him feel uncomfortable if he didn't make any of those fancy speeches that all the chits seemed to expect today. He was primarily a country type of man, more concerned with the drainage of his fields than the cut of his coats, but the importance of marrying an acceptable girl and setting up his nursery had been strongly borne into him by his uncle and benefactor, the Earl of Arkwright. Like most bachelors, Arkwright was a strong believer in duty and family as the sovereign code for everyone around him. He had made it quite clear that he wished to see Longstreet settled, and with a hopeful family, before becoming an earl himself.

Until Miss Stanhope-Fredericks, there had been no woman to whom Longstreet could talk about the really important things, which to him meant horses, hounds, and hunts. All in all, he was quite pleased to find himself with Miss Stanhope-Fredericks, one of the rare females who had no nonsense about her and talked his language. She wasn't a bad looker, either; not a patch on any of the accredited beauties, but her face was pleasing and pretty and her eyes had the nicest way of crinkling up when she laughed. Her mouth was a bit small, but full, and nearly always smiling. He especially liked her hair—it was dark brown and glossy, exactly the shade of his favorite hack during his short time at Cambridge. Indeed, Lady Mickleham and Mrs. Stanhope-Fredericks would have been most happy could they have known what thoughts rattled about in Sir Rupert's mind.

Those august ladies would have been less pleased had they been able to follow Phillipa's mental activities. Having met Sir Rupert casually a time or two at various hunts, she had sized him up pretty accurately. On the field he was a bruising rider, a leader, and off the field he was a dead bore. True, she was grateful enough to sit this dance out with him, to chat horses and sip lemonade, but the primary cause of this emotion was the fact that her feet were killing her. The pretty green dancing slippers, which looked so adorable with her gown of pale-green satin, topped with a floating froth of darker green sarcanet, were unbearably tight.

Phillipa had never been so glad as when her first Season was over and she was no longer constrained to wear white exclusively. Most of the debutantes in the ton looked delicate and virginal, clad solely in white, but Phillipa, with her mane of dark-brown hair and pale skin had looked, as Letty—her best friend and a devotee of Mrs. Radcliffe's Gothic effusions—had said, quite wraithlike. To this Phillipa had laughed and invited a closer inspection of her considerable height, saying that without a doubt she was the most Junoesque wraith ever seen.

That same romantic Letty now sat, disconsolately, not far from the dowagers, where she had been deposited by a young man with just a shade too much alacrity before he went to search for a livelier partner. Letty—who was properly styled Lady Lettice Winterthorpe, the only child of the Duke and Duchess of Connaught—knew that she had no conversation and was a poor dancer, defects that not even her fair fortune could override in the eyes of most men, and which made it all the more surprising that she had been chosen by Phillipa Stanhope-Fredericks as a bosom bow. Unbeknownst to Letty, Phillipa's championship had begun merely as a charitable action, the same as she would bestow on an abused animal or servant, and had surprised both the principals by developing into a deep and lasting friendship.

"Here you are, Letty. I don't blame you for sitting this one out. The heat is truly incredible, don't you agree, Sir Rupert?" Phillipa lazily seated herself on the tiny chair to Letty's left. "Do you object if we join you, Letty? This is closer to the windows and perhaps some vagrant breeze will be so kind as to visit us."

"Might I be so privileged as to join your little party? Lady Lettice . . . Miss Stanhope-Fredericks . . . Longstreet . . ." The manners were correct to a shade, giving Letty the proper precedence as the lady of rank, but the warm smile and twinkling eyes were all for Phillipa's benefit and she smiled in return.

"Alvanley! We would be most honored to have you join us . . . please be seated." As usual, Phillipa took the lead, knowing from experience that if one waited for Letty to say anything, one waited a long time.

"My thanks. 'Tis quite a crush, isn't it?"

"Yes, especially with London so thin of company this early. Poor Aunt Beatrice was in quite a dither about whether there would be a sufficient turnout to keep her from disgrace."

"My dear Miss Stanhope-Fredericks, having known your lady aunt these many years and holding her most high in my affections, I quite refuse to believe that

16

she would ever be in a dither about anything—wars, crises, let alone anything as paltry as a party, even one as magnificent as this. Surely she must realize that she alone is responsible for the dreadful state of the roads for a week past, which were positively clogged with carriages and berlins hurrying to Town so as not to miss Lady Beatrice Mickleham's party."

Phillipa laughed gaily. "I am afraid you know our family too well, my dear sir. Modesty and reticence have never been two of our besetting virtues," she said, which brought an answering laugh from Alvanley and a slow burn of anger to Longstreet's dull wit.

Frippery fellow, he raged inwardly, disliking Alvanley's easy manner and cavalier attitude toward Miss Stanhope-Fredericks's family. How polite and well-bred Miss Stanhope-Fredericks was to sit there and continue to talk that silly Society chatter with the fellow when he knew she would much prefer to be comparing the relative merits of the Quorn against the Cottesmore. If only she didn't have to toady to such a dandified fop. If only he had the right to protect her from such impertinences. . . . Yes, Lady Mickleham and Mrs. Stanhope-Fredericks would have been most gratified to know the drift of Sir Rupert's thoughts.

Unaware of the imagined slights being heaped on her head, Phillipa asked. "Am I to assume from your presence that we are to be honored with an appearance by the Regent tonight?"

"It desolates me to deny you anything, Miss Stanhope-Fredericks, but poor Prinny has been captured by his ministers after a long and eventful chase and for the moment is fulfilling his duties as Regent."

Sir Rupert's temper rose another degree. The Prince

of Wales was far from the ideal of a leader, but he was the reigning monarch and the generations of loyalty bred in the sturdy knights of the house of Longstreet did not appreciate levity concerning the head of state. Fortunately for both Longstreet's social future and Alvanley's about-to-be-bloodied nose, Lady Mickleham's impassive butler, Summerhill, swung open the great doors to the dining room with an almost theatrical flourish and announced in stentorian tones that supper was being served.

Almost at once Phillipa was besieged with gentlemen, all types of gentlemen, to Letty's wondering eyes and Longstreet's growing jealousy—an incredible array of gentlemen, young, old, fat, thin, short, tall, handsome, plain gentlemen, all clamoring for her attention. Phillipa handled it with her usual aplomb, settling the question of who would go into supper with whom and seeing that no young lady was neglected.

Letty would have given anything to be able to handle both herself and other people like that, to be able to make herself so well-liked, and said so to her friend the next morning, only to be shocked speechless when Phillipa pronounced the whole thing a dead bore.

They had agreed to ride early, both to blow away the cobwebs left by the party the night before and so as to have the park fairly well to themselves, and had met at what the fashionable world would call a disgracefully early hour. Letty, long schooled to Phillipa's unpredictable moods, was aware that her companion was restless and, as their grooms had dropped back to a respectful distance, she waited for her to elaborate.

18

It was almost a quarter of a mile later at a dead walk before Phillipa spoke again. "I thought it would be different this time, Letty."

"What would be different?"

"Society. I thought that once we were no longer the new debutantes—the 'fresh crop,' as Ronnie would call them—it would be fun, not like before, more . . . oh, I don't know . . . just different."

Letty was unable to ingest this bit of heresy. She was not at all clever or popular like Phillipa, but last Season she had had an enormous amount of fun and had innocently supposed that since Phillipa had been doing so much more, that she had had a proportionately larger share of enjoyment. "I don't understand."

Wisely Phillipa let the subject drop. They chatted of the ball, of who was there, and of who was and was not speaking to whom.

"Oh, Phillipa, look! Isn't that Mrs. Valelyn coming toward us?" Letty's voice was tinged with dismay.

"Yes, it is. Dare we be uncivil and pretend we haven't seen her? Odious creature . . . she probably wants to read a very polite peal over my head for her lack of an invitation to Aunt Beatrice's party last night."

Dexterously the two girls turned their horses with a casual ease. The object of their displeasure, a florid matron in her thirties, whose sole aim was to establish herself in the highest ton no matter what it took to do it, saw the ploy and hardened her heart against the girls for the slight. Everyone knew that Lady Lettice was a fool and would follow whoever was leading, but as for Phillipa Stanhope-Fredericks, going along with her nose in the air like that and for all her money

19

being just a plain miss, just as she, Honoria Valelyn, had been, it just wasn't to be borne. Hardly knowing that she had done so, Phillipa had made a dangerous enemy.

Unaware of her plight, Phillipa at last reined in and looked casually over the Park. "I think we've lost her. And I don't think she saw us see her. Shall we go back? The Park is starting to fill and if we do not return immediately, we shall be accosted by everyone and held up for simply hours."

Letty agreed quickly, for as much as she loved Phillipa and wished to emulate her, horsebacking was not her favorite pastime. It was rare for Phillipa to give up either time in the saddle or the prospect of a long chatty visit with some of her more lively friends, and Letty said so.

"Am I so obvious, then?" Phillipa said, laughing, negotiating the traffic that surrounded the Park with ease. "Well, the truth must obviously come out. Arnold's birthday is next week, and I am making him some handkerchiefs. Thank Heavens my embroidery is well enough so that at least the initials will not disgrace him. Poor mite; he complains so about the food at Saint Gregory's that Cook is making the most enormous box of all his especial favorites—candies, cookies, even a plum cake. After being so spoiled I fear that the discipline of school life is difficult for him."

"How fortunate little Arnold is to have a sister who cares so much for him," Letty murmured with the envy only an only child could know.

"I suppose our situation is unique. Poor Mother was so ill after Arnold was born. I played mother to him, that is, when I could get him away from Kirky—our nurse—and that has probably made us closer than the norm. Ah, here we are. Shall I stop here or go with you to your house and return?"

Being with Phillipa had given Letty a kind of second-hand courage, assumed so that she should not disgrace her friend. "No, there is not the slightest need, for as you know, we are only two squares over. Get on upstairs and begin your sewing and I shall be all right. Lister is with me."

Phillipa bade her friend an affectionate farewell and slipped to the ground, giving the reins to the groom. Squaring her shoulders against a tedious task, she marched into the house and inspected the early bouquets sent by last night's admirers, startling a little at the size and number of the ones from Sir Rupert. If this kept up, the hall would look like a greenhouse before noon. The butler was instructed that should anyone call, Miss Phillipa was unable to receive, being prostrate with the headache. Before the bell could ring again, Phillipa dashed upstairs to clean up and spend the afternoon wrestling with needle and linen.

CHAPTER TWO

Even to those who knew her intimately, Eustacia, Duchess of Connaught, was an imposing figure. Not so much in size, for it had once been boasted that a man could span her waist with his two hands, but one soon forgot her diminutive stature when confronted with her indomitable will. It was a source of never-ending grief that the sole offspring of her brilliant marriage was a soft wiffle-waffle girl who took after her father's easy ways, and since the duke's crippling accident there was no chance of an heir.

"Letty, is that you?"

Letty paused in the hall and gave up all hope of getting to her room unobserved. She dreaded these sessions with her mother, for at the end of them she always felt like a fool. "Yes, Mamma."

"Come in and have some chocolate with me."

Entering her mother's boudoir, Letty pulled the bell for another cup according to a time-honored custom, then planted a quick kiss on the proffered cheek and retired to a chair by the fireplace, far enough away that Eustacia should not be overly bothered by the smell of horse.

In looks they could have been sisters, Letty being

but a pale copy of the original, who, sitting propped up in bed, looked completely untouched by marriage and motherhood: pale blond hair formed an aureole around the cherubic face, which was marred only by a pair of mannishly cold blue eyes. There was a distinct resemblance, but anyone seeing Letty would have called her passably pretty; anyone seeing Eustacia would have forgotten Letty altogether.

"You modern girls! Up riding so early! After a ball like last night's I would have been prostrate for hours."

"I was not tired, Mamma, and Phillipa wished to ride early."

"I noticed that you were not dancing last night, my pet. Were you saving your strength for this morning's ride?"

"No, Mamma. I was not dancing because I was not asked."

Eustacia took a sip of chocolate and considered her daughter's words. "Perhaps you should choose your friends more carefully. I noticed last night that you spent a lot of time with Miss Stanhope-Fredericks."

"Phillipa is my friend, Mamma."

"And friendship is a very valuable thing to have, providing that it is with the right people."

A silent servant, well schooled in the ritual, brought Letty a cup of chocolate, which she sipped absently, burning her tongue. "Mamma, you cannot mean to say that Phillipa is the wrong kind of person . . ."

"You must let your mamma decide what is right and wrong, Letty. Now we wish no scandal or gossip to arise from this, so a sudden drop would be out of the question, but I do want you to start right now to see

23

less of Miss Stanhope-Fredericks. Within a few weeks you will have grown apart and with no talk attached."

"But, Mamma! I don't wish to lose Phillipa as a friend."

Eustacia raised her eyes with a show of shock. At one time, Letty would never have dared cross her, even in such a mild way as this. No, there were great things afoot for Letty and she could not be putting up her will against her mother's now. Sitting up in bed, Eustacia turned the look on her daughter that had made strong men crumble and dowagers of the first stare give way—the mouth set, the cold eyes glittering.

"Lettice! I do not intend to argue the point. I have given you an instruction and you will obey it. As your mamma I know best and I will not have you challenging me."

As expected, Letty wilted. It did not occur to her that she could do anything else, for her mother had given Letty her orders. To obey was her duty.

In another room, small, dark, and smelling of lamp oil and cooking odors, far from the perfumed salons of London, duty was also under discussion, though under a completely different set of circumstances. The plain plaster walls, adorned with smoke and candle smut accumulated over generations, the rude furniture, the rush-strewn floors and unglazed windows all bespoke a peasant dwelling of low estate, while the two men, though dressed in rough clothing and in a state of hygiene best not discussed among polite society, were obviously of the gentry.

The younger of the two lounged easily on the rude

camp bed, watching the movements of his companion, a man a few years his senior, packing a small valise, very much hampered by a barely healed wound. No word of complaint escaped the thin lips, however, and the younger man thought too much of his own skin to be so foolhardy as to offer assistance. Even his mother would have been hard put to identify Lord Ronald Mickleham as he lay at ease now, dressed in the shabby clothing of the peasants and with a full two weeks' growth of beard.

"How long do you think you will be gone?"

His dark-visaged companion stopped and leaned heavily on his cane. "I don't know, Ronnie. As long as need be, I guess. According to Aunt Theodora, Father is pretty broken up and I must do what I can to comfort him as well as seeing what I can do to clear up Laurence's death. It's a damnable world when nine-year-old boys die mysteriously, Ronnie."

Unable to reply, Ronnie nodded. He knew how fond Ludlowe had been of his little brother.

"Hightower has agreed to let me help in the investigation. I haven't been in England in a long time, so he thinks I would do best in an undercover capacity."

"Like here."

"I think that influenced him. Anyway, he said he'd give me the complete plan when I got there. Funny—asked me what grades I'd had in school."

"School? Fellow's barmy."

"Perhaps, but he's one of Father's oldest friends, and the way he stepped in to help when we got the news about Laurence. . . . All in all this trip home is a good thing. I've been away a number of years now

25

and Father needs me. I can't really do any good here, not with this . . ." He gestured bitterly toward his wound.

Lord Ronald was silent as his friend continued to pack, slowly, painfully, and considered how much he owed this man and yet how little he knew of him. Lord Paul Geraint Ludlowe, called Pablo during their late escapades, was potentially one of the wealthiest young men in the kingdom, a man of impeccable breeding to whom the highest doors of the ton opened gladly. Yet he fought in the Peninsular War like the veriest foot soldier, taking dangerously foolhardy assignments and seemingly reveling in pieces of wildness like the trek they had just completed. Disguised as peasants, the two friends had spent at least a fortnight behind enemy lines, gathering information, even on one memorable occasion entering Marmont's camp undetected in the guise of beggars.

"You're awfully quiet, Ronnie."

"Am I? Sorry. Just thinking about some of the scrapes we've had. I'll miss you, Pablo."

The dark head shook sadly. "No, merely Paul Ludlowe now. Pablo died by a French bullet." A careful hand massaged the barely healed wound. "But they were splendid, weren't they? The sort of thing that happens only to a very few. And I will miss you too, Ronnie. Well, that's the lot. If you're going down to the quay with me, we'd best go."

Acting on the shared impulse that had saved them so many times in the past, as if their minds were one, each stuck out his hand and grasped the other's warmly in the grip of a brother.

26

"I have to go home to Greathill first, but in time I'll be in London. Castlereagh will doubtless expect a personal report. Can I do anything for you while I'm there?"

"I'd take it kindly if you'd call on my mother when you have time . . . and in London, if you go out any, sit out a dance with my cousin Pia. You might like her. She's not in the common way."

Ludlowe grinned, the white of his teeth startling against his sunburned skin. "Still trying to match me up with that infernal cousin of yours? I tell you I dislike her already. Since you're selling her so hard, she is probably a beanpole . . ."

"She is tall."

"And ill-favored. And with a squint. And poor as a church mouse."

"Not that. My uncle Augustus is fairly plump in the pocket. Enough to bail me out a time or two when I was a young fellow and in a bit of a scrape. . . . Not the sort of thing a gentleman can explain to his mother, you see . . ." Ronnie returned with perfect amicability, for this exchange had been enacted so many times it had taken on the air of a well-loved ritual.

"I confess I am shocked, young Ronald! Still, if you promise not to mention your cousin Pia again, I promise to be civil to her should we meet." Again Ludlowe tried for lightness and, failing, clasped Ronnie to him in an embrace of camaraderie known only to those who have been under fire and through danger together. "Take care, my dear friend. Now—let us go, for the tide will turn soon."

CHAPTER THREE

Augustus Stanhope-Fredericks was basically a simple man. A good landlord, a bruising rider, a devoted husband and loving father—though not necessarily in that order—and when at home at Worthington Grange he counted himself a happy man, away from the organized insanity of London Society. Didn't these London people ever sleep? One returned home from a ball at a most incredible hour, fell exhausted into bed, and then was waked up impossibly early after what seemed just a few moments' sleep by the chatter of morning callers and an influx of bouquets from his daughter's besotted beaux. By eleven o'clock the place was awash in flowers and the smell . . . ! Flowers were all very well and good in their place, growing in the wild, or even a few in a vase on a lady's boudoir table, but when they took over the hall in acresful, it was too much.

It seemed that not even the library was a safe haven for Augustus that morning. Fanchon announced that Sir Rupert Longstreet had called and wished to see Mr. Stanhope-Fredericks. As Longstreet had featured prominently in the last lecture about Phillipa's future read him by Beatrice, Mr. Stanhope-Fredericks was familiar with the name and had a fair idea as to the purpose of his visit.

"Your servant, sir." Sir Rupert bowed most correctly. He had dressed carefully for this meeting, changing clothes quite three times before being satisfied with the result: rich but not opulent, restrained but not sober, fashionable but not foppish—hopefully what a man would want a son-in-law to be.

With a careful eye Augustus inspected his visitor. He was a man just out of the first flush of youth, sturdy and muscular, but who would probably run to fat before many years were gone, unfortunately attired in clothes that seemed to emphasize his stockiness, but not displeasing to the eye. Thanks to Beatrice's briefing, Augustus also knew about his prospects: in a very few years this young man would be an earl. It could be very nice to have a wealthy earl in the family, if Phillipa fancied him. Longstreet was not what Augustus would have chosen for his daughter, but he would have no objections to him, and his wife and sister-in-law had brought in to him rather strongly that Phillipa did not seem to disdain Longstreet's company.

"Good to see you, Longstreet. Can I offer you some refreshment?"

Sir Rupert shook his head, suddenly nervous, and wished himself a thousand miles away. "No, thank you, sir. Mr. Stanhope-Fredericks, I have come to talk to you about the future of my fondest hopes . . ."

"Thought it might be something like that. Sit down, won't you?"

"Thank you, sir. Now as you know, I have been fortunate enough to have made the acquaintance of Miss

Stanhope-Fredericks, and have spent a fair amount of time in her presence—enough to know that I would be most honored if she would consent to be my wife." There! He had actually said it without any mistakes, and almost immediately he began to feel better. The die was cast.

After the prescribed amenities Mr. Stanhope-Fredericks nodded and rose to bow courteously as Longstreet bumbled his way from the room, managing to hit an inordinate number of things on the way out. Despite the eligibility of the match, Augustus found himself hoping Phillipa would turn Longstreet down, yet surely that was a prime piece of folly. Good name, good blood, good fortune . . . but he wanted something more for her, like the something he saw in Arabella's eyes when she looked at him, even after all these years.

"Augustus!" She was reclining on her couch, but reached forward to kiss him sweetly, more beautiful to him now than when he had first met her.

Phillipa was there too, perhaps not a beauty like her mother, but too good, Augustus suddenly felt, for that horse-mad country bumpkin who was going to address her. He bent to kiss her proffered cheek. She had been reading to her mother, one of their favorite pastimes together.

"What brings you up here this time of day, Augustus? Not that the sight of you is not most welcome, but it is unusual. Now you are usually hiding out at your club with other men under siege of the Season."

Mr. Stanhope-Fredericks laughed and took his wife's hand. "And so I should be, had I not had a visitor."

30

"A visitor? Who?"

"He concerns Phillipa more than either of us, my dear. Phillipa, today Rupert Longstreet came to ask permission of me to ask for your hand."

"And did you give it?"

"Of course. He is a most eligible parti."

Arabella positively glowed. "Longstreet! Beatrice was right when she said she had never seen a man so smitten."

"Do you like him, my child?" Mr. Stanhope-Fredericks asked.

"I find him an amiable enough companion, Father, if one wishes to talk of horses and farms," Phillipa said softly.

"He said he would return this afternoon to put the question to you."

"Phillipa, love, wear the sapphire dress this afternoon and be sure that my maid does you hair carefully. It must be fetching, but not contrived. Something suitable for a future countess . . ."

Augustus cautioned his wife that nothing was settled yet, that Phillipa must think, and she replied that of course she had to think but it was best to be prepared, wasn't it, as she had been prepared for a declaration from him—right down to dress and earrings—at least three times before he got around to proposing. He disclaimed any knowledge of such goings-on, and in the middle of the loving, sprightly discussion Phillipa rose and slipped out unnoticed.

CHAPTER FOUR

Phillipa, dutifully prepared with dress and earrings but without an answer, put a warm smile on her face and walked into the drawing room. Unfortunately, Sir Rupert did not make a very felicitous impression on Miss Stanhope-Fredericks. She was fond of him and found him both kind and amiable, but the sight of that stocky worthy clad in garments suitable for a man ten years younger and two stone lighter made her pause. Kindness and amiability were all very well, but for such lukewarm qualities could she commit the rest of her life to living with such a creature as now stood before her? Somehow she had always thought there would be something more, something better. . . .

"Good afternoon, Sir Rupert."

"Good afternoon, Miss Stanhope-Fredericks . . ." Sir Rupert said, and his carefully prepared oration dried up, leaving him bereft of speech. Later he would wonder what would have happened had he been glib of tongue and able to continue with his role at that particular moment.

From outside there came the sound of the bell and Fanchon's measured tread. Cravenly Phillipa hoped that it was an unfashionably early caller, someone to save her from this predicament, but Fanchon passed by the drawing room doors, going on to the library, where Phillipa knew that both her parents sat awaiting the outcome of her conversation with Sir Rupert.

"Bought a new hunter at Tattersall's yesterday," Longstreet said more confidently, retreating to familiar ground once they were seated. "Big rawboned brute. Freddy Appleyard said he's the ugliest bonesetter in England."

Phillipa smiled.

"Hoping to have a good hunt season this year . . ." Blast it all, here he was, refusing his fences like a greenhorn. Up and over . . . "Miss Stanhope-Fredericks, as you may have noticed, my attentions to you have been most marked and after talking with your esteemed father I have been led to believe that you would not be averse—"

The earl-to-be's proposal remained unvoiced, cut off by the sound of a piteous cry. Alarmed, Phillipa said, "That's Mother," and flew out of the room, all thoughts of her poor suitor forgotten. She was not to think of him for several days, and then only to wonder vaguely how long he had waited. Sir Rupert would have been greatly chagrined to know just how little of his beloved's attention he occupied, even at the best of times.

Phillipa's worst fears were allayed on entering the library, for both her mother and father were alive, though Mr. Stanhope-Fredericks was shockingly pale and Mrs. Stanhope-Fredericks was convulsed in the grip of some spasm.

Mr. Stanhope-Fredericks spoke through thin, blood-less lips. "It's Arnold. I just heard from the school. He's . . . he's dead."

Mrs. Stanhope-Fredericks's spasm had been more than merely a symptom of shock. For weeks she hovered between the world of the dead and the world of the living, clinging somehow to both. Phillipa and her father nursed her devotedly, submerging their own sorrow to give strength to her, and at last their efforts were rewarded by the doctor's pronouncement that, barring some unforeseen setback, Mrs. Stanhope-Fredericks would recover. Somehow the holiday season had passed without notice and the world outside lay in the grip of winter, but the doctor's diagnosis was Christmas and spring all rolled into one.

Augustus Stanhope-Fredericks's happiness was short-lived, however. With a hand that shook from too much indulgence already, he poured another glass of brandy and read once more the letter from Sir Percy Hightower that had lain for weeks amongst his neglected correspondence.

My Dear Tiny—

Word has just reached me of your tragic loss. I cannot say how deep my grief is for your sake, but to my everlasting sorrow I must give you further pain. It is my fault that we have grown apart in recent years, we who were so close at St. Gregory's, but nothing has ever made me wish more that we had kept in contact. As you may know, I have been on the Board of Governors of St. Gregory's for some years and in the past few months a steady flow of reports has been coming in regarding certain criminal but unprovable irregularities at the school. Had I but known that your son was at the school, I could have warned you, or done something. . . . We have an agent in the school at the moment, but to gather any admissible proof will take time. My dear old friend, your grief is mine. I remain

Your childhood chum,
Cubby

With a cry of frustrated rage, Mr. Stanhope-Fredericks flung the missive into the fire and, weeping, began a long diatribe against those who murdered children. He was still raving, brandy-mad, when his daughter, investigating an unusual night noise, found him, and being unwilling to let his valet see him in such an unaccustomed condition, she cajoled him into going to bed.

Mr. Stanhope-Fredericks, although not a teetotaler, was nevertheless a temperate man and, while the contents of the letter were indelibly cut into his brain, the brandy fumes had wiped out any memory of a verbal indiscretion, leaving him free to vow in all good conscience that no one would ever know of this secret horror.

Slowly Mrs. Stanhope-Fredericks grew stronger and, as Phillipa had borne the brunt of the nursing, her father decided that she could use a little pampering. So it was to be that while her parents took the waters at Bath, Phillipa would have the sovereign treat of being once again placed under Kirky's care, this time at Ivy Cottage, where the old nurse had retired to live with her sister, Amanda Selkirk. Rest, freedom from nursing chores, and good country air would be just the thing to perk his little girl up again, Mr. Stanhope-Fredericks thought. He could leave her under Kirky's care and never worry a minute about her.

CHAPTER FIVE

Eustacia, Duchess of Connaught, had never looked lovelier. Triumph of her will over others had always been a flattering cosmetic for her and now, sitting with the Duke of Lowood and knowing the reason for his call, she positively glowed. It was a testimony to her strength of purpose that when she looked at His Grace she saw not an elderly, wizened, rather unpleasant-looking man with ferretlike features, but the finest collection of precious gems in the Polite World, four estates fit for a reigning monarch, and the third largest fortune in England. And now, she thought, it would be under her control, through Letty, and of course Letty was nothing but a cipher anyway, especially since that Stanhope-Fredericks girl had left town.

"Letty, my dear . . ." Eustacia said in honeyed tones. "Do come in. I believe you are acquainted with His Grace, the Duke of Lowood?"

Letty stood at the door, poised as if for flight. She had met the duke a time or two and he had always made her feel uncomfortable, as if he could see through her clothing.

Eustacia, in spite of her smiling face, was furious at her daughter's obvious terror and lack of animation. Really, if the girl didn't breathe occasionally she might just as well be a dressmaker's dummy! Conversely His Grace of Lowood saw Lady Lettice's silence as a sign of a good quiet nature and a biddable disposition. He saw her as one who could just as easily be dominated by a husband as a mother.

"Good afternoon," Letty murmured.

"Come here, child. I have marvelous news for you," Eustacia purred, savoring each word with an unholy triumph. "My dear, you are the most fortunate of young women. In the absence of your poor father, His Grace has come here to ask me for your hand in marriage, and I have of course accepted."

Lady Lettice was quite unlike her mother. Looking at His Grace, she saw not his possessions or his status, but instead his slitted lips, two dry, clawlike hands that would now have the right to touch her, to own her. . . .

With an inarticulate cry, Letty dashed from the room, fleeing to her bedchamber. She had not accepted Lowood's offer, but that would make little difference. Between His Grace and her mother her fate was sealed, for the bargain was struck as far as they were concerned, though some small part of her mind kept saying that as long as she had not agreed it wasn't real. Not that her saying or not saying anything had ever really affected any of her mother's plans for her.

The thought of those thin, dry hands on her flesh set Letty to pacing frantically, as if their owner had been seated next to her. She could not live with Lowood, be his wife, have him touch her. . . . She would kill herself first. Perhaps if she went to her father . . . ? No, she could not hope for help from that quarter. It was as if the accident that had broken the duke's back had broken his spirit too. There was no one, no one . . .

Letty stopped short. Phillipa. Of course, Phillipa. She was still in mourning, but she would surely advise her, despite the enforced cooling of their friendship. How wonderful it would be to have Phillipa's sane, brave advice! Letty immediately sent a letter along to Phillipa.

My dearest Phillipa—

The worst has happened. Mamma has betrothed me to the Duke of Lowood. I know he offered for you last Season and of your refusal, so you will surely know what emotions grip me now. I cannot rely, however, on the chance that my refusal will be accepted, and so it seems my fate is sealed. Oh, my dear friend, I cannot bear it! Mamma keeps talking on about his houses and the jewels I will wear, and all I can see are his eyes, his ugly, cruel eyes. I have thought of going on to Coombs Farm and begging my father for

38

protection, but that would probably be worse than useless since he now lives in retirement and lets Mamma do as she will, but I must do something! Please, please . . . Advise me what to do.

Desperately—
Letty

Phillipa read the letter over twice, her anger mounting with each word. What a foul world this was that allowed the death of young children like Arnold and the persecution of sweet innocents like Letty by such a creature as Lowood! Her memories of the old satyr, with his dry, grasping hands and leering expression, were vivid enough to cause real concern for Letty. Mr. and Mrs. Stanhope-Fredericks had been a staunch bulwark against Lowood's advances, and even with that his courtship of her had been a difficult time for all; Letty was being shoved into his arms by her mother . . .

Poor Letty! Poor Arnold! Phillipa agonized for the ones she loved, wishing that there were something she could do.

Phillipa stopped in the center of the room, brought to a halt by an idea so fleeting and so audacious it was almost frightening. She had often thought, since the receipt of the hideous news from Headmaster Snodgress and even more so since the night of her father's indiscreet rambling, that there was something havey-cavey about Arnold's death and that if she could only get there, she could discover the truth. Now, unknowingly, Letty had given her the chance.

It just might work. Her parents and Letty would

think her safe at Ivy Cottage. The ladies Selkirk would think her safe at Coombs Farm with Letty. Letty would never correspond with the ladies at Ivy Cottage and in the middle of the deception Phillipa would be free to go as she liked. In a few days, when she had finished at St. Gregory's, she could return to Ivy Cottage from her "visit to Coombs Farm" and no one would be the wiser. It would work!

Then. . . . Full of imaginary triumphs, Phillipa's mind ran on. Not even the Duchess of Connaught could hope to have a full Society wedding in less than three months, for such haste would cause talk. That would leave at least eight to ten weeks for Phillipa to think of some way to help Letty. It could be done, it could be done! She could have laughed aloud.

Time was important now. Hastily she scribbled a note in reply to Letty, full of encouragement and appeals to her bravery, hardly thinking of what she wrote, merely trying to give her friend a little boost in return for the precious gift of the opportunity of freedom. Finished, she rang impatiently for Maggie and bade her bring in the message-carrying stableboy.

"Thank you for waiting. Here is the reply for your mistress."

A grubby, ill-kept paw took the missive and shoved it into a capacious and undoubtedly filthy jerkin pocket. "Thank'ee, mum."

"Lady Lettice is indeed fortunate to have someone like you to depend on." This was it, now or never. Phillipa took a deep breath and spoke in rapid low tones. "I too want to help her ladyship, but I need your assistance. At the closest coaching inn you can find I want you to send back a carriage and four with two postboys for me. They are to say that they are from Coombs Farm. Do you understand?"

He nodded. "Yes, mum, but . . ."

The parlor door swung open to admit the ladies Selkirk. Phillipa groaned inwardly. If only she could have had a few more moments! The stablehand, already thrown off balance by the strange errands of the day, was thrown into a near panic by the imposing presence of the elder lady with the hard eyes.

"Miss Stanhope-Fredericks! I cannot approve of the guests you choose to entertain in my parlor and especially unchaperoned! Who is this person?"

With an effort, Phillipa forced herself to speak gently to the elder Selkirk lady. Now was no time to blow the whole game with a temper fit, tempting though it was. "I merely asked him to wait while I penned a reply to his message. I am afraid I must leave you."

Kirky's lower lip trembled and her gentle old face crumpled like crushed paper. "Oh, my dear . . . your mother . . ." She stood like a shadow behind her formidable sister.

"No, no, Kirky, dear . . . nothing of the sort. It is my dear friend Lady Lettice Winterthorpe. She has been ill," Phillipa said, improvising freely, trusting to Heaven and the discretion of the stablehand, "and is recuperating at her home, Coombs Farm. She very much desires me to visit her."

Mrs. Selkirk sniffled fluently. "Obviously she does not know you are still in mourning or she would not invite you to a house party . . ."

"It isn't a house party, Mrs. Selkirk. There will be only Letty and me there along with her father, the Duke of Connaught. He never leaves Coombs Farm since his accident. I assure you all is proper. Letty merely wishes my company during her convalescence."

The mention of a duke had a miraculous effect on Amanda Selkirk. "It is most irregular; however, I suppose that something can be arranged."

Phillipa was quick to press her case. "I knew you would feel that way. A carriage will soon be here."

Mrs. Selkirk frowned. The whole affair seemed badly planned, but then everyone knew the Connaught ménage was a ramshackle affair; still a duke was a duke, and Amanda Selkirk was never slow to better herself in the world.

"Very well. It seems a shabby way of doing things, but if the girl really needs you, it is only Christian charity that you go to her. I shall chaperon you personally."

With fading hopes Phillipa watched the determination in the older woman's face. She was as trapped as ever. Then, amazingly, Kirky came to the rescue.

"My dear, you forget the vicar and the Sewing Society for Charitable Cases are coming tomorrow. It is your meeting . . . you were going to discuss duty."

A rare parade of emotions marched across Mrs. Selkirk's face. It had taken a long time and the leadership of the little group had been hardly won. "You are right, Hepzibah. I had forgotten. You will have to go in my stead."

"Oh, no," Phillipa sighed, then quickly followed with, "I would not dream of pulling Kirky out on such a trip. You know her disposition toward travel sickness."

"Travel sickness is merely in the mind," said Mrs. Selkirk.

"It is not," said Kirky, a trifle pale at the remembrances of past indignities, for even the best sprung of carriages driven at a moderate speed caused her the most extreme of agonies. "Amanda, dear, might we not send Maggie? After all, Coombs Farm is not very far away and as the gathering isn't a social one, I cannot see where we would be amiss."

Although this was far from what she had wanted, Phillipa was wise enough to realize that this was the best she was going to be able to get. "Thank you, Kirky. That sounds ideal!"

Seeing herself outnumbered, Mrs. Selkirk nodded. "Very well."

After achieving the supreme triumph of escape, however hurriedly, Phillipa felt able of doing almost anything; not even the presence of Maggie, not the uncomfortable antiquity of their coach, could dampen her spirits. Admittedly Maggie was a problem, for Phillipa had not planned to have any accomplices, but perhaps it was for the best.

"Maggie, how do you feel about adventures?"

The servant girl's brow wrinkled. "Adventures, miss?"

"Yes. Like in books."

"I can't read, miss."

Phillipa made a small sound. This was going to be difficult.

"But Cook can, and she reads me the loveliest stories. All about knights and beautiful ladies and dragons . . ."

It was simple after that. Phillipa spoke carefully,

choosing exactly the melodramatic words that would guarantee the maid's loyalty. At the end of the recital Maggie was her slave. Then Phillipa began to speak of what she intended to do and Maggie went pale.

"A maid? You, miss? But you can't! You're a lady."

"But I can pretend to be a maid. It can't be that difficult."

"Oh, miss, you just can't! It wouldn't be fitting. There are things . . . things best not talked about, but you just can't go to a boy's school. I've heard tales of things that happen . . . a lady just isn't safe!"

"I shan't be a lady, I shall be a maid."

"That's all the more reason not to, miss," Maggie said, but her passionate pleading left Miss Stanhope-Fredericks all the more determined. When it became apparent to the young maid that her mistress was determined beyond all reason, she gave up trying to dissuade her and instead began a course of instruction.

For a servant girl to become a lady is a difficult task, it is said. For a lady to become a servant girl is infinitely more taxing. A lady must strip away layers of pride and culture that have been bred into her line for centuries and revert to the basest layers of Society. The instructions seemed endless: Never look a superior in the eye; curtsy to everyone from the housekeeper up, including the governess and companion; never answer back, even if you are right; never show pride, except to be in the service of your employer; never mention anything personal; never question an order, no matter how idiotic it seems; never be obtrusive; never exhibit ideas above your station; never speak unless spoken to.

Phillipa's head began to swim.

Still, Miss Stanhope-Fredericks proved to be a willing pupil and by the time the coach arrived at Pelton Lea and the best inn was found, Phillipa had a fair idea of the life of a serving maid. It sounded extremely distasteful. Still, distasteful or not, it would have to be faced. Arnold was dead in that place and no one was even making inquiries, let alone doing something about it. Her mother was an invalid, requiring all her father's attention. Kirky merely sat and wept under the disapproving eyes of that dragon she called sister. Lady Mickleham had her own business to do, grieved though she was over Arnold's death. The trustees of the school—well, no outcry had been raised, so they couldn't be doing anything. That left only her, Phillipa thought. It was a daunting idea, but the blood of warriors ran through her frail female veins and she resisted all of Maggie's entreaties to give up the masquerade and return home.

Later that night a tense and wakeful Phillipa, tormented by night fears and the unrelenting snores from Maggie's truckle bed, walked the room and, her imagination fed by the lurid novels of the day, dreamed of untold horrors. What would await her after Maggie had been sent on to the Grange?

She had lighted the bed candle without fear of waking Maggie, for the servant girl was so sound asleep as to be dead. Oh, to be able to sleep like that, with no troubles and no cares, no responsibilities! Phillipa thought it might be a good thing to be a servant, even for a short time, if they could sleep as soundly as that.

Finally she fell into a restless doze and dreamed of the first view of St. Gregory's.

CHAPTER SIX

The sight of the kitchen garden alone almost discouraged Phillipa. It had run to seed years ago and now only a few of the most determined plants managed to survive among the weeds. From the front, the school was unprepossessing and modestly shabby, as befitted a respected establishment for turning the young sons of minor gentry into gentlemen, but from the rear—which, of course, visitors would never see—it was a horror. Originally built during the reign of the Merry Monarch, probably as the manor house of some petty lord, the building was a cream-colored stone edifice three stories high and determinedly square. In later years, probably when it had become a school, a hastily constructed ell had been added in the center of the back facade, a two-storied excrescence of mismatched stone and timber, whose door opened directly into the ruined garden without even the amenities of a porch or shed.

At the bottom of the kitchen garden Phillipa could see the stables and a few outbuildings, all surprisingly small for a place of this size. At the far end of the ruined lawn, quite far from the house, was a distinct rise in the ground, almost like one of the queer antique funeral barrows or a foundation for some sort of folly. To the right side of the building, hidden from the front by a hedge, was what was once a rose garden. Some of the hardier specimens had survived the neglect and doubtless in summer would perfume the air with scent. In late April, however, the touch of spring had not yet fully come and all but a few stalks stood bare against the elements, snarled by the wind into fantastic shapes, choking the flagged walks with their prickly branches. Only a few blossoms had incautiously dared to open their petals.

Finally Phillipa pulled her cloak more tightly about her, picked up her poor bundle of belongings, and marched across to the scabrous wooden door, whose faded paint flaked under her knocking fingers. She had to rap twice before the door opened, revealing a rectangle of blackness from which poured a flood of odor so strong that for a moment Phillipa had to fight to hold her stomach calm. It was a sick stench of rotting filth and . . .

"What be ye wantin' here?" came a booming voice from the darkness, strangely sexless in its tone and timbre.

"If you please, I'm looking for work . . ." Phillipa whined.

"There be no work here," said the voice, and the door began to close.

"Please, mistress . . . I've walked far. . . . Have you nothing I could be doing?" Phillipa stepped into the darkened hole of the doorway, ready to throw her weight against the door if necessary.

Another voice, light and thin as a child's, floated

out of the blackness. "We do be one short, mum, since Hannah died."

The door ceased its pressure against her shoulder but opened no wider. "All we be needing here is a scullery."

Phillipa gulped. This was not quite what she had had in mind. "If that is all you have . . ."

"Ye never be a scullery!" The door opened slowly, as if to afford a better view of the stranger. Phillipa took advantage of this and stepped boldly in, if nothing else, glad to be out of the chill wind.

The kitchen was not as black as it had appeared from the outside. Two small windows let in a bit of watery sunshine, just enough to show the filth and dilapidation of the room. In the middle of one wall was the fireplace, fully big enough for a man to stand in, equipped with cranes and hooks for cooking and apparently not cleaned nor swept in the past generation. The center of the room was dominated by a huge table of bare wood, completely covered in dirty dishes. Two doors, both closed, filled the wall to Phillipa's left. There were low tables against the back wall, scored with the usage of years and not very clean. The fourth wall, opposite the dresser, had yet another closed door, flanked by a wide, grimy dresser that held but a few pieces of thick pottery. Phillipa was able to take in almost everything with a single glance, including the greasy state of the flags and the piles of refuse by the door, but her attention was riveted on the two women.

The elder one held the door; a large, burly woman, she could have masqueraded quite easily as a blacksmith, for only her old-fashioned skirts and scrawny knot of hair from which a disreputable cap hung, dirty and askew, proclaimed her as a female. Two small dark eyes stared with undisguised hostility from that vast, doughy face. Her dress, which had once been dark blue, was now a vivid multicolor from spills and stains, the full skirt cut in a style that was twenty years gone, and from the olfactory evidence it would seem that during that time the dress had never been removed, nor it or its owner washed.

The other female was little more than a girl, scrawny and thin to the point of emaciation. Her state of cleanliness was little better and the strands of hair that escaped from her dirty cap were tangled and greasy. The tiny, pinched face was devoid of expression, blank as an idiot's, and it was not long before Phillipa learned that such a look could come just as easily from physical exhaustion as mental incompetence.

"I can be a scullery," Phillipa said softly.

The giantess surveyed her with a grunt, taking in the cloak and dress borrowed that morning from Maggie, her soft hands and pale face, the soft brown hair scraped back into a serviceable knot. "Ye niver worked belowstairs in yer life. This is a good house. We need no fancy women here. Ye can just get on with ye!"

Phillipa made her decision instantly. She was going to stay no matter what. With a delicate sigh, she slid into a faint.

"Oh, mum, she be dead!" howled the young one. "I seen people die afore . . . she be dead!"

"Shut up, ye silly wench. She only fainted. Probably been no better than she should have been and expects to stick us with her by-blow. Run fetch Mr. Snod-gress. He'll know what's to be done with the likes of her. Hurry, gel!"

There was the sound of scurrying feet and the slamming of a door. Phillipa lay quite still, wishing she had chosen a more comfortable site to fall. The flags were rough and greasy and there was a chill draft from the partially open door playing around her back. She could not risk moving or opening her eyes. If her ears had not told her that the older woman was still in the room, her nose would have.

The creature began to speak and it was a full minute before Phillipa realized that the old woman was praying! The low drone of words was an extemporaneous exhortation to the Lord to protect her and her house from any Devil's spawn looking to cause mischief. It was a good thing that Phillipa was summarily immobilized, for she would have been hard put to choose between tears and laughter at such a performance. To imagine the impertinence of the woman, importuning the Lord for all as if He were squire of the county! It seemed somehow indecent.

"Well, well, what's this?" The voice was cold and somehow sly. Phillipa thought that the girl she was pretending to be could die right there on the flags at that moment and there would be no warmth, no regret, no human emotion in that voice.

"She's dead. She just fell down dead. I've seen people die afore, and she fell just like they did. . . ." said the young one, whining.

"Shut up, Florrie. None of yer nonsense! Back to yer work!" bellowed the older woman, and in a moment there was the splash of water and a muffled whimper. "Drat the gel—not good for anything!"

"Now, now, Mrs. Manning, we might have something better in store." With a long, inbred caution the headmaster studied the face of the fallen girl. Very few things that happened could not be turned to the advantage of a clever man was one of his mottoes, and Ira Snodgress considered himself a very clever man. "Let us not make our decision too hastily, Mrs. Manning. You say she asked for work?"

"Yes, but she be no servant! Look at her hands. Soft and white . . . she'd not last a day."

He strode up and down the kitchen floor, his shoes making a path quite near Phillipa's face. "What do we have? A pretty young girl, quite obviously not a kitchen helper, begs for work here at an isolated school when there are easier, cleaner jobs to be had a scant mile away in the village."

"Send her away, Mr. Snodgress! The boys . . . she'll bring us nothing but trouble."

"No, think if you're capable of it, woman! Think! She must be in hiding from something or someone and as long as we offer her sanctuary she will give us her loyalty. Fetch some water. I will talk to her." The headmaster grinned. He enjoyed having power over people.

Phillipa was glad to hear that she was at last to be "revived," but she was unprepared for the flood of stale-smelling liquid that drenched her face and shoulders.

"Well, gel, have ye a name?"

Standing, Phillipa swabbed at her face with a

hanky, pushing back dripping strands of hair. "I be called Maggie."

Seen for the first time, Mr. Snodgress was anything but impressive. His age was indeterminate. The frizzy hair that surrounded his face like an obscene halo was gray, but the face itself was strangely devoid of age. It was a sly face, a cunning face, with piggy little eyes and an ungenerous slit of a mouth.

"Well now, Maggie," he said, rocking on his heels slightly for emphasis. "Mrs. Manning tells me you want work. Is that true?"

"Yes, sir," she murmured, remembering to lower her eyes humbly.

"Where have you worked before?"

Phillipa had thought of that one. Of course it was out of the question to say Worthington Grange, so she had decided to appropriate Aunt Beatrice's country home. "Lakelands, sir. Two days' journey from here."

"And what was your position there?"

"Under-lady's maid. I was the assistant to Lady Mickleham's maid," she said, blithely inventing.

"And so you left the post of under-lady's maid to come seek work as a scullery. Fascinating!" He was like a fox, working in on a helpless chicken for the final kill. "Quite a change, wouldn't you think, Mrs. Manning?"

The dragon's mask hardened. "Send her away, Mr. Snodgress, back to her own kind. She's no good."

"Please, sir, I just want honest work, that's all."

"Now, girl, no one leaves a good job for a dirty one without a reason. Tell me why."

Phillipa had not anticipated this. "I quarreled with Hastings . . . Lady Mickleham's maid . . ."

"And you were turned off without a character?"

"Yes, sir."

"For one quarrel with her maid she turned you off without a character?" His question hung accusingly in the air.

"Can't ye see she's no good, Mr. Snodgress? Flaunting her pretty ways . . . Women like her make men forget the path of God. . . ."

There was an incredibly long silence that stretched Phillipa's nerves almost past bearing.

"Mrs. Manning," Mr. Snodgress said finally, his reptilian eyes never leaving Phillipa's face, "this girl will do. Set her to work. Tomorrow tell me how she has done."

"Ye'll rue the day she came here, Mr. Snodgress. Mark my words, she'll bring the Devil into this house. I've tried to keep this a Christian establishment, with no fancy women or idleness, but—"

"Silence! I'll hear no more on the subject. Come to my office tomorrow and give me a report," he snapped and walked from the kitchen without a backward glance.

"Ye asked for work, missy! Ye'll get it. Aye, ye'll get it," Mrs. Manning rumbled ominously. If indeed idle hands were the Devil's playground, this pretty servant of his would soon have no time to play at all. There was room only for godliness in her kitchen, be it the last bastion of the true Christianity on earth!

CHAPTER SEVEN

Nothing ever learned in all her schooling or in London Society helped prepare Miss Phillipa Stanhope-Fredericks for what she learned that day. Being new and consequently suspect by Mrs. Manning, she was not allowed to help serve, but only to scrape the plates as they came back from the noon meal. It was a poor meal for schoolboys, being naught but bread and hard-smelling cheese and the butter for the bread all but rancid. Phillipa could not remember the exact sum her father had sent each quarter for little Arnold's tariff, but it had been exorbitant, which made this unpalatable offering all the more inexplicable.

It became her lot to carry out the refuse from the table and floor, the plate scrapings, the dishwater jellied with congealed grease, on and on and on until it seemed that she had carried out everything in the kitchen that was not part of the foundations, every step watched by Mrs. Manning's unrelenting eyes. At last, with a parting exhortation not to stop, the cook swept from the kitchen and almost immediately cleared the air by her absence.

"Best to sit down for a moment now," said the tiny

Florrie, speaking her first words since Mr. Snodgress's appearance in the kitchen so many hours ago. With a quick, ungraceful motion she lowered herself into a sitting position on the damp flags.

Groaning, Phillipa sat gingerly on the floor, not caring if it were damp or dirty. Not even the worst throw she had ever taken in the hunting field had caused her this much pain.

Florrie smiled, exhibiting blackened stumps of teeth that would have seemed appropriate in a raddled crone, though Phillipa suspected that the girl was probably the younger of the two.

"Take it soft, Maggie. It be hard work, harder than most."

"Yes, that it is. Did you do it all yourself?"

She nodded with the stoic simplicity of a beast of burden. "Since Hannah be gone. She was the other girl. There's never been more than two."

And she had died, Phillipa thought. *Another death in this horrid place.* "When was that?"

"Oh, it be gone two, three months now." Florrie sniffed inelegantly and rubbed her nose against a filthy sleeve. "It were the fever. Maggie, be it truth ye was a lady's maid?"

"Yes."

The dull eyes glowed and for a fleeting moment Florrie looked close to her real age. "Tell me . . . is it true that ladies wear unmentionables with lace on them?"

Taken aback, Phillipa thought involuntarily of her own belongings, scattered between Worthington Grange and Ivy Cottage and with the real Maggie,

55

wherever she happened to be at the moment, all dripping with convent-made lace. "Yes, sometimes two or three kinds."

Florrie laughed, a dry, crackly sound like crushing winter leaves. "Oh, if I had things like that, I'd wear them on the outside, not the in, because it would be so pretty."

Phillipa was caught between tears and laughter at such naive ignorance, but she held her tongue, knowing that dreams in an arid place such as this were far too precious and fragile to shatter.

"How many boys are there?" she asked instead.

"One and sixty. There be three instructors: Mr. Lovelace; Mr. Pettigrew; and the new one, Mr. Catton. He's ever so handsome." The thin voice was wistful.

"Three instructors. Does the headmaster hold any classes?"

"Mr. Snodgress? Aye, some, though he prefers just being master. Mrs. Manning is the housekeeper—that's the title she uses, but she does the cooking too." Florrie stood up. "We best be getting back to work. She'll be back any minute."

Florrie's warning had been none too soon, for no sooner had Phillipa begun in a semblance of work than the housekeeper stalked into the room. Miss Stanhope-Fredericks had faced some of the legendary dragons of her time and station, including a few patronesses of Almack's, but nothing had prepared her for a creature like Mrs. Manning.

Before the afternoon had progressed very far, Phillipa had become convinced that the woman's knowledge of housewifery was nonexistent or that she was

56

criminally negligent. The flour and meal were alive with vermin, the milk clabbered even in the pitcher, cockroaches as big as a human hand walked unafraid across the floor, although neither Mrs. Manning nor Florrie seemed to notice that anything was out of the ordinary.

Arnold had been sent here, Phillipa's mind kept repeating; her spoilt, adored little brother had been sent to this place of horrors and here he had died. *Why? Why?*

"Come." Florrie came back into the kitchen from carrying in the tureen of mush, grabbed Phillipa, and almost dragged her out the back door. "While Mrs. Manning be serving the supper we gets a bit of a break."

Muscles trembling with pain and exhaustion, Phillipa seated herself gingerly on a brick curb. Above, the sky was delicately tinted by the fading sun; how much had happened since that same sun had risen!

"Tell me, Maggie, be it true that ladies has candles in their rooms every night?"

Phillipa's mind jumped to the comfortable suites that she called hers, where a dozen tapers were always waiting should she desire them lit, a potent defense against her dislike of darkness. "Yes, usually both candles and lamps."

"Cor, can ye picture it? A candle any time ye'd be wishing for it." Her face was rapt with visions of untold luxuries.

"Don't we get candles here?" Phillipa asked with a sudden new fear.

The servant girl's reply was a derisive sneer. "A candle? Sooner ask for gold. Candles cost money and they's too good to waste on the scullery. Anyway, there's nothing to stay awake for here. Not unless the monitors come around."

"Monitors?" The term was vaguely familiar, mentioned in letters from Arnold. He had been complaining about their roughness . . .

"Older boys they be, seniors that help oversee the school. They patrol the halls, watch at meals, and keep the tads in line."

Just like a prison, Phillipa thought.

"Florrie! Maggie! Idle sluts!"

Both girls jumped, guiltily aware of being caught in the wrong. Mrs. Manning, wrathful as a thundercloud, stood in the doorway, wiping her hands on a food-streaked apron. "Gel! Wash them dishes now and be sure they's clean. Florrie, ye'll be taking the tray tonight."

Wide-eyed, Florrie nodded and followed Mrs. Manning's bulk and jingling keys through a heavy door and down a half-flight of stairs into what, from Phillipa's point of view, appeared to be a series of storage rooms. Apparently with her coming Florrie had been shoved up a notch to more pleasant duties.

Florrie soon emerged from the larder, arms full of foodstuffs, followed by a red-faced and puffing Mrs. Manning. While Phillipa continued to wipe the dishes, her companions proceeded to prepare a second meal, smaller than the first, but much more succulent looking. Bacon, ham, potatoes in some sort of white sauce, and other dishes were concocted with incredible speed, sending forth aromas that made Phillipa's head swim. Back at the Grange she would have turned up her nose at such common fare, but compared to the mush that was on the stove awaiting their supper it appeared positively ambrosial.

The housekeeper, unlocking yet another cupboard, fetched a thinly plated tray of enormous size, the silver coating so worn away as to reveal large areas of base metal, and then arranged food, dishes, utensils, and clean plates, covering the whole thing with a cloth.

"Now, take that to the front first-floor parlor, and don't delay. Lay the meal and come right back down. None of that lazing around."

"Aye, mum," Florrie gasped, her frail frame grossly distorted by the gigantic laden tray.

The light faded into a soft glow in the sky that would not pierce the gloom of the kitchen. Only when it became too dark to see one's hand did Mrs. Manning bestir herself to light an oil lamp, a small one on the worktable, the tiny, greasy flame totally inadequate for such a sizable room.

Florrie returned, alarmingly pale, the now empty tray hanging by her side. Phillipa's heart went out to the pathetic creature. The trip bearing the loaded tray had been too much for her, for she was now coughing, her thin frame shaking pitifully.

Taking no notice, Mrs. Manning rose to dish out the remaining mush into three plates, setting them at the empty end of the table. Florrie and Phillipa took their seats, one on either side of the housekeeper, who watched them with baleful eyes to assure proper behavior.

"Bless this house, O Lord," Mrs. Manning intoned commandingly. "Keep the inhabitants safe from mischief-makers who would do us harm. Protect Thy servants and ensure their faith and pious behavior . . ."

At last the housekeeper finished and without a pause attacked the congealing mush as if it were the greatest delicacy in the world. Florrie too ate determinedly, shoving in the food with marvelous precision. Phillipa's own hunger had fled earlier in the day, but she forced a few spoonfuls of the mess down.

Not a word was spoken during the strange meal and the instant Mrs. Manning had swallowed the last mouthful she was on her feet, carrying the plate to the washing pan at the other end of the table. To Phillipa's amazement Florrie rose immediately as if she were attached by some invisible cord, a strange wraithlike shadow to Mrs. Manning's gross bulk, and then motioned frantically for Phillipa to do the same. Apparently, Phillipa decided while washing their utensils in the now cold water, no one was allowed to continue eating after the amount of time Mrs. Manning deemed suitable to consume a meal had elapsed, for she would doubtless condemn any pleasure in taking a leisurely time over the table, once the bodily necessities had been attended to.

After the trip upstairs to reclaim the dirty dishes, which again left Florrie coughing and pale, she began to dry and stack the clean crockery while Mrs. Manning checked the cabinets and locked the larder and storage rooms, taking the key from the huge ring that hung where her waistline had once been. Phillipa's only thought, other than remaining upright, was to stay close to the light, for, dim as it was, it was some protection against the cockroaches she could almost hear crawling forth under the cover of darkness.

"Come then," Mrs. Manning said and most astonishingly dropped to her knees. Florrie too knelt and motioned Phillipa to do the same.

"Dear Lord . . ." Mrs. Manning intoned again, her deep voice resounding strangely through the dark kitchen. On and on she went until Phillipa feared her knees were bleeding from prolonged contact with the rough stone floor. At last the housekeeper finished, rising ponderously at the last amen. "Don't dawdle," was her only comment as Miss Phillipa Stanhope-Fredericks struggled with stiff and screaming muscles to rise.

Following the faint gleam from the low light she carried, the two girls kept close to Mrs. Manning's bulk, Phillipa for one trying to breathe as little as possible. Mrs. Manning turned abruptly from the corridor and began to climb an enclosed flight of stairs that was incredibly steep and narrow between two clammy stone walls. At the final turn the steps became ladderlike and Phillipa had to grasp the rough walls to maintain her balance.

"Now, get to bed and no gossiping, for I can hear ye, as ye well know, Florrie. There is a lot to be done tomorrow, the Lord willing."

Stumbling with weariness, Phillipa followed Florrie into the attic. Two pitifully thin mattresses lay on the floor, undignified by as much as a sheet. A none-too-clean blanket lay folded at the foot of each one. Phillipa's pitiful bundle sat at the head of the pallet nearest the window. Apparently Florrie had taken a few precious moments during the day to rush up here with Phillipa's belongings.

Without warning or nighttime benediction the door slammed shut, plunging the room into terrifying darkness. Miss Stanhope-Fredericks lay across the musty mattress and pulled the blanket up, resolutely ignoring thoughts of the previous occupant.

Florrie shook her again and Phillipa awoke unrefreshed, for one frightening moment unable to move. Dirty gray light seeped through the encrusted windowpanes, giving the shabby attic a ghostly, unreal look.

"Best get up now, Maggie. It's most half past and we'd best be getting downstairs. Mrs. Manning's knocked twice now."

"Half past what?" Phillipa asked vaguely.

"Five, of course. We need to set breakfast at half past six and there's water to draw and the meals to cook and wood to cut. . . . Come, gell"

The day was a ghastly mirror of the one before: the labor, the smells, the inedible mush, the prayers. During the few times the housekeeper was away from the kitchen Florrie talked, and an unbounded flow of words carried on her thin voice, as if they had been long stored up and merely awaiting a recipient.

Miss Stanhope-Fredericks survived her second day at St. Gregory's more through the charity of her fellow servant than through any strength or courage of her own, for she was exhausted to the end of her abilities. The strength of the little slavey was phenomenal to Phillipa's eyes—carrying enormous loads, then racked by a furor of coughing, then picking up another burden, seemingly without stopping. At bedtime, when Miss Stanhope-Fredericks had to concentrate on each step, she was amazed to see that Florrie moved with the same measured tread.

In the few minutes before sleep claimed her, Phillipa made and discarded many plans for getting into the records office, but she was effectively trapped in the scullery and just as far away from the truth as she had been in London. It was a depressing thought, and to the accompaniment of Florrie's coughing, she slid into a dreamless sleep.

CHAPTER EIGHT

The tears flowed freely, and even had she tried, Phillipa could not have stopped them. She huddled in the protective tangle of the neglected rosebushes, swiping at her eyes with her sleeve. Frustration, anger, and physical exhaustion had combined into a wave of emotion that could only be expressed in a freshet of tears.

"Are you quite through?"

Angered and embarrassed, Miss Stanhope-Fredericks sprang to her feet, head high and eyes flashing. "How dare you, sir! To watch me in such a private moment!"

Dark eyes widened in surprise; from his vantage point behind the girl she had appeared to be nothing out of the ordinary, simply a servant girl in a dirty garment, weeping like a watering pot, but now neither her face nor her demeanor suggested anything connected with the servants' hall. Smiling lazily, the man continued to stare. "I believe you are in error, my girl. I was calmly sitting here, perusing the grandeur of nature . . . even in such a primitive state . . . when you came almost to my very feet and prostrated yourself, making the most unbelievable noises."

From Florrie's description this could only be the new history master, for he was very handsome: dark eyes; dark hair; skin slightly sallow from a fading sunburn; and cheekbones and a jawline that could make a romantic cry for happiness. The only thing to mar the picture of masculine perfection was the cane he carried to support a favored leg. Against her will Phillipa drew in a sharp breath and the thought of Sir Rupert Longstreet vanished from even the smallest recess of her brain.

"My apologies, sir," she said with the iciest hauteur possible, turning to escape to the haven of the scullery. "Mrs. Manning will be wanting me."

"That won't do. She is currently with Mr. Snodgress, I believe, and will be so for some time. Don't worry," he said, partially misinterpreting the hesitation in her eyes. "I shan't attack you. Rose gardens in such a condition as this are not meant for seductions. Sit there."

Phillipa obediently took the seat he indicated, unable to repress a small smile. Oddly enough, she did feel safe with him and for one fervent moment wished to be wearing almost anything save the rag she had on.

"Are you sure this is proper? You're a gentleman and I'm just a scullery . . ."

"I see nothing wrong with it," he said, leaning cautiously against a ruined trellis, his hands busy with a pipe. "Gentlemen and servant girls have been talking for generations, but you're no more a scullery than I. What is your name?"

"I am called Maggie."

"Maggie . . . suitable." He puffed a cloud of smoke, more affected than he cared to admit by a pair of blue eyes. "I am the history master and my name is Geraint Catton."

"Geraint? What an odd name."

"It's Welsh, like my mother. I suppose I should feel fortunate she didn't saddle me with one of their more outlandish names, thirty-eight letters long and half of them doubled."

Phillipa giggled in spite of herself. She had not expected to find such a handsome, agreeable companion in such a place and the thought of the noisome, reeking scullery vanished from her mind.

"That's better. Such a solemn face you were wearing. I'm glad to see you can laugh." His lips still held a smile, but the dark eyes grew cold and Phillipa experienced the queer feeling of walking on treacherous quicksand. "Now, Maggie, you may call me a curious man, but I would like to know what a girl of your caliber is doing in a place like this. Surely there were other jobs to be had, more suitable to your station."

Phillipa had to look away from the penetrating gaze. She stood. "I must be getting back."

"Of what are you afraid, Maggie?"

Steady blue eyes met dark ones. "Afraid? Of what should I be afraid?"

"I wonder," he said, not bothering to stop her departure. "I just wonder."

Luck was with Phillipa, for the housekeeper had not returned in her absence. Florrie still dozed by the fire, and seen in repose, her face was startling. Framed by lackluster hair drooping from a dirty cap, the tiny, pinched face looked a death's-head, the eye sockets great dark holes burned deeply into the flesh. Phillipa felt a rush of remorse. She had been so occupied with her own problems she had had no time or energy to spare for another creature. Florrie had even taken part of Phillipa's work on herself and Miss Stanhope-Fredericks made a solemn vow that when she left this hellhole the little slavey would come with her. Surely there were doctors who could make her well again.

The respite did not last, for eventually Mrs. Manning returned, her humor unimproved by the meeting with the headmaster. She apostrophized Florrie as a lazy slut and Maggie as the Devil's handmaiden, sent to lure the innocent into idle ways.

The noon meal was a poor affair of dry cheese and bread, and Phillipa's heart twisted in bitterness when she thought of the life young Arnold must have led here. His letters had complained of the food at St. Gregory's, but—Heaven forgive all of them—they had merely thought it the measly whining of a schoolboy.

Florrie, bent double with coughing, carried out the serving of the boys' luncheon. After her departure, Phillipa became very busy in straightening up the counters and sweeping the flags, aware of the value of action around Mrs. Manning. Any slow movement could be interpreted as encroaching sloth, any response save blind obedience as evidence of sass and back-talking.

The front doorbell, mounted on a rusted spring above the door, jangled with a tired sound. The struggle of the housekeeper's conscience was written across her face; smeared with dough from fingertip to elbow, she was in no condition to answer the summons, but her helper was occupied with feeding the pupils.

"Well, don't just stand gawking like a ninny," she snarled at last. "Answer it, but see you come straight back here!"

Head high, Miss Stanhope-Fredericks swept through the door out into the unknown reaches of the front hall.

"Well, ye certainly took yer own sweet time, I must say!" The voice was as totally absurd as the body from which it originated. High and piping, it arose from a chest that should have sent forth roars of Falstaffian proportions. Absurdly fat, the short man bounced into the hall, droplets of perspiration rising on the vast expanse of white brow. Quickly beady eyes ran over Phillipa in an action oddly reminiscent of a sporting skirter sizing up a horse, leaving Miss Stanhope-Fredericks feeling both uneasy and vaguely dirty. "Oh, ye be new. And certainly a change from that other gel . . . a most welcome change." A still unfamiliar smile rearranged the pale face.

Phillipa ignored the longing to slap that soft, silly face and lowered her eyes. "Florrie was busy, sir."

"A great improvement! Well, don't just stand there gawking, gel, tell Mr. Snodgress that I am here." With a mincing walk that he no doubt thought the first stare of elegance, the stranger showed himself into the drawing room.

Without a thought to the consequences, Phillipa took the opportunity that was offered. Who knew when she would have another chance to explore the upstairs with such relative impunity? She fairly flew up the thinly carpeted steps and barely avoided a collision with the history master. Inwardly Phillipa swore furiously at the loss of precious time and attributed her quickened breathing to the climb.

"Well, Maggie! I haven't seen you in these regions before."

"I was sent to the door, Mr. Catton."

A flicker of emotion danced over the chiseled features. "A visitor? What a rare occurrence." A slow smile transformed his face and he reached out to push back a lock of hair that had escaped the confines of her cap. "That ridiculous piece of headgear doesn't flatter you, you know."

"My cap? It is quite the latest thing among the Order of Scullions, I assure you, sir. We should be desolated to appear without one," Phillipa replied saucily.

"You are indeed an original, my girl, which makes me wonder." He extended a careless forefinger to her chin, studying her face with the praticed eye of a connoisseur. "What would bring you to a hole like this? You are more than a tolerable-looking girl, even in that dress and that atrocious cap. I'd wager that properly costumed you could appear at Carlton House without attracting undue notice."

Phillipa shook with outraged feminine vanity; she longed to tell him that she had attended several functions at the Prince's residence and had been hailed as quite a beauty. Somehow it seemed very important to have this Apollo know of her triumphs, no, not Apollo—more a spawn of Vulcan, with his dark aspect and the cruel lines chiseled deeply around his mouth.

"Excuse me, Mr. Catton, but could you tell me which is Mr. Snodgress's office? I must not leave the gentleman waiting."

"A gentleman?"

"More of a tradesman that a gentleman, I should say," Phillipa's ready tongue said, blithely forgetting all vows of caution under the steady scrutiny of a pair of dark eyes.

"A tradesman. Hmm. You'll find Snodgress's office at the end of the hall," Catton said abruptly and stalked on down the stairs as best his injured leg would allow, leaving a startled young woman behind him. Of all the women he had known, why did his blood have to be so disturbed by a pretty-faced scullery maid with the manners of a duchess?

CHAPTER NINE

Unaware of the turmoil she had caused, Phillipa stepped into the upper hall. It was a short passage, darkly panelled and ill-cleaned. At the end were a set of double doors, doubtless added by some owner in the past years with pretensions to grandeur. Once the legend HEADMASTER—KNOCK BEFORE ENTERING had been lettered proudly, but years of neglect had reduced the gold to mere smudges.

"Come in."

Mr. Snodgress's appearance had not improved since their last meeting. Phillipa made a quick glance around the room, noting the bookcase, the worn red drapes, the enormous desk from several generations ago.

"There is a gentleman to see you, Mr. Snodgress, in the parlor downstairs."

"A gentleman, eh? We must go down and see him. What are you doing up here? I thought Fanny, or whatever the tiresome chit's name is, was supposed to be up here."

Phillipa remembered to forget her training in etiquette just in time to let him pass in front of her and go out the door first. "Florrie is ill, sir. Mrs. Manning sent me to answer the door instead."

"Ill? What ails the wench?"

"She coughs, sir. Dreadfully."

He stopped and stared for a moment at Phillipa. "Coughs, does she? Send Mrs. Manning to me, girl. The gentleman and I will take tea in the parlor."

Feeling quite satisfied, Phillipa walked back to the kitchen, where Mrs. Manning looked up from the breadboard, her eyes bright with growing fury. Florrie again huddled near the fire, spasms of coughing twisting her fragile body.

"Well," snarled the housekeeper, not breaking the rhythm of her kneading. "Ye took yer own sweet time. What was ye doing?"

"There was a gentleman who called for Mr. Snodgress. He told me to fetch him immediately," Phillipa said with sweet reason, forgetting that reason and fanaticism were mortal enemies.

"And ye went upstairs? Without permission? Insolent slut!" Without even bothering to wipe her hands, Mrs. Manning sent a startled Phillipa sprawling on the rough, dank stones. "Let that be a lesson to ye, wench."

Miss Stanhope-Fredericks sat up slowly, feeling under the dough that had been transferred to her cheek to where a bruise would doubtless come later. "Mr. Snodgress told me to tell you he wants tea, Mrs. Manning. For two, in the parlor." It was an effort to speak.

"Tea! And why didn't ye tell me sooner? Up, lazy gel! Florrie, stop drowsing and come with me. Maggie, get down the company china."

The two of them disappeared into the storage area, the keys on Mrs. Manning's belt jangling, and when she emerged it was empty-handed. Florrie followed, her frail frame bowed by an enormous and distinctly hideous silver service, doubtless the gift of some long-ago class. After securely locking the door behind her, Mrs. Manning made the tea with her own hands, then swept out with the laden tray.

The time seemed much too short before Mrs. Manning charged into the room again. "Brazen hussy!" she roared, swinging a ham-sized fist that Phillipa barely managed to avoid. "And what Godless wiles did ye use? Ah, I rue the day ye ever set foot in this place, I do. Y've been naught but trouble. The Devil himself is in ye, with yer pretty ways and wanton face! Well, no matter what the master says, ye'll not be pulling any of yer fancy tricks under me nose! Hear?"

Phillipa could not only hear but smell, as the housekeeper had planted herself quite closely, her small evil eyes gleaming wildly, her breath rancid. With noble effort and bearing Miss Stanhope-Fredericks of Worthington Grange faced her back squarely. "I do not understand you, Mrs. Manning. What is it I am supposed to have done?"

"That's what I'd like to know. I serve tea to the master and Mr. Dinsworthy and all of a sudden the master tells me that Florrie is to be kept in the kitchen and ye are to do all the front work instead. What wiles did ye use, ye saucy wench?"

"None. I merely answered the door. I used no wiles."

"Aye," she rasped. "And dinna think ye'll be using any, either, for I'm going to be watching ye." Her ravings dropped to a steady trickle of muttered invectives and she turned back to her bread.

Phillipa swept half-heartedly at the floor with a disgrace of a broom, pondering the boon Fate had thrown her way. This was almost a carte blanche to search in the front regions; no one could question a maid's appearance in the office area at any given time if she belonged there. On the other hand, if they had found out her true identity in some way, if they were only waiting for her to trap herself, that carte blanche could be a death trap. It would be so simple for them to allow her to hunt about and then BOOM! A prowler shot in the night—how tragic that it was only the housemaid—but what on earth was she doing up on the first floor at that hour of the night? How sad.

The service bell jangled imperiously and with a snarl Mrs. Manning looked up from shaping the loaves. "They be wanting ye to clear the tea things. And come straight back here, understand?"

Phillipa hurried into the front hall, where faintly she could hear the boys chanting their lessons. It was strange, she reflected, that in a boys' school she should have seen so little of the children. With a pang, Phillipa wondered if she would be able to see the maroon and gray uniforms at close range without breaking into tears. Arnold had been wearing one the last time she had seen him and no doubt he had been buried in it.

The parlor was not empty; Mr. Snodgress and his visitor, Mr. Dinsworthy, still lounged in the shabby chairs.

"You may clear the table," Mr. Snodgress said, indicating the service with a magnificent sweep of his arm. All at once he seemed transformed from a rather greasy headmaster to a genial country squire. "What is your name again, girl?"

"Maggie, sir."

"Ah, yes, yes . . ." Pulling every last fragment of enjoyment from the situation, the headmaster stroked his chin. "Dinsworthy, Maggie was a gift to us. Merely walked up to the door one day and asked for work. It was only our Christian duty to help her."

Dinsworthy responded with a singularly nasty chuckle. "At the least, at the least. I only wish it had been at my humble abode. But"—here his voice lowered to a very ineffectual whisper—"is she trustable? We don't want any problems."

"We shan't have any. She was grateful of the place. Pretty little thing, no? Old Manning is quite put out over her! Was once a lady's maid." Now was the moment. Ira Snodgress cleared his throat and prepared to play benefactor. "Maggie?"

73

"Yes, sir?"

"I want to inform you that I have decided that you are to take over the front duties. Florrie is, as you've informed me, too ill to meet the public. Mr. Dinsworthy and I both agree that you are much too pretty to be kept in the kitchens." His reptilian eyes gleamed coldly over a mechanical smile. "Now take away the tea things. Florrie will show you the routine for a day or so and then we'll see how you work out."

CHAPTER TEN

The dining room was of immense and singularly ungraceful proportions to Phillipa's searching eyes; a long room furnished solely with rough tables and benches. Great draperies of cobwebs lurked in the high corners and there was a thin but definite coating of grime over everything. The soaring windows were uncurtained and the panes positively filthy. Phillipa could not have even guessed how long it had been since the floor had been scrubbed.

The two girls placed the plates and spoons on the plank service table. "Put the spoons first, nearest the edge," Florrie instructed. "That way, if a boy bumps the table and a spoon falls off, nothing happens 'cept a scolding. If a plate falls off it breaks, and the boy gets sent to the punishment box."

"The punishment box? What's that?"

If possible, Florrie went even paler. "Best forget ye ever heard of it, Maggie."

"But what is it?"

"It's where bad boys are sent . . . in the back," the little slavey said grudgingly, her hands busy.

Phillipa nodded, amazed at Florrie's reaction. If indeed it were anything more than a bogey-tale made up to scare the boys and silly serving maids, the punishment box would bear investigation.

"Now, when the boys come, they're to be in line and quiet—no talking is allowed at meals, save for prayers."

"How do I ensure that?"

She laughed nervously. "Ye don't. That's the job of the monitors. Ye just stand here and dish out the victuals and ye can't say nothing. Remember that, Maggie. Ye don't want the monitors down on ye. Now the dipper be in the kitchen; bring it when ye brings the porringer. Ye stands here and the boys files past and ye puts the gruel in the bowl—just the same to each, one dipperful and no more."

"But that ladle is barely half a bowlful! Surely there must be more than that for the lads."

"There's bread," Florrie said, as if surprised that one should ask for more. "One slice apiece. No one gets more, but ye don't really have to worry about that. The monitors'll make sure the boys behave. We must hurry now."

They worked quickly, carrying out the rest of the

75

crockery and silverware, and finally the tubs of suspicious-smelling butter. At last Florrie looked at the preparations and nodded. "It won't be a minute till the bell rings. Mind ye, Maggie, not a word to the boys."

"Why?"

"Mr. Snodgress forbids them talking during meals. He says they'd be rowdy otherwise."

Almost as nervous as at her first Court presentation, Phillipa waited by Florrie's side behind the table and watched as the great door opened for the boys to troop in, their faces downcast and silent save for the soft scraping of their shoes on the floor. Like little gray and maroon ghosts, they queued by the table, taking a spoon and a plate and waiting. With a sense of horror Phillipa saw the deadness of their eyes, the almost total lack of animation in those pinched little faces, and found herself wondering if any of the boys knew how to laugh.

Florrie tugged surreptitiously at Phillipa's sleeve when they entered, but she needed no warning. Standing out from the crowd of faded schoolboys as hawks among lovebirds, the monitors strode among the children like lords among peasants, enforcing their law with cruel jabs and blows, usually against the smallest boys. Twice only Florrie's restraining hand stopped Phillipa from flying into battle against those uncouth beasts with no more weapon than the gruel ladle.

Until now Phillipa had harbored some vague notion that these monitors were some sort of older students, working their way through school. The sight of these young men, however, dispelled any such idea, for not only were they obviously not scholars, they were indubitably basely born in the bargain.

"Hey, Alf! Look here at the new serving wench!" The three monitors crowded about the table, causing Phillipa discomfort and Florrie absolute terror.

"Where did ye come from?"

"What's yer name?"

"Can't ye talk?"

"A dummy, by God!"

"Cat got yer tongue?"

"Away, all of ye!" The great reverberating voice shook the very floor. Respectfully the monitors parted and Phillipa looked curiously to see who, besides Mr. Snodgress, could command obedience from such ruffians.

A young man approximately her own age strode forward, his exaggerated air of command almost as ludicrous as his clothes. A great loutish lad, he would have been none too good-looking no matter what he wore, but in the dirty finery of a dandy in a style three years gone, he was positively laughable. Unfortunately, Phillipa saw him only as he was at the moment and was unable to appreciate the distances he had come since being born the fourth son of a professional beggar and occasional tinker from the wilds of Lancashire.

"Ye are causing a disturbance. Neither meself nor Mr. Snodgress will be allowing anything like that."

As if by magic the monitors dispersed, knowing the voice of their master. Impudent eyes raked Phillipa. "What's yer name, gel?"

"Maggie."

77

"I am the head monitor. My name is Seth. Ye will say sir."

There was a lengthy pause before the "sir" issued from between Miss Stanhope-Fredericks's clenched teeth.

"Good." Abruptly he was gone, leaving Phillipa unsure and shaken.

Florrie tugged gently at her sleeve. "Let's go, Maggie," she murmured, barely audibly. Her face was chalk white.

Mrs. Manning did not look up as Phillipa carried the near-empty porringer over to the stove, trying to forget that in a short while that disgusting gruel would be their supper.

"Well?" the housekeeper asked.

"She did well," Florrie said.

No word of commendation would be forthcoming; that was against her principles. Wearily Mrs. Manning stood and jangled her keys. "Come along, both of ye."

The storage rooms were oubliettelike cellars in the oldest part of the house. From the kitchen door the way went down a flight of slimy steps into a series of rooms dug into the earth itself. No glimmer of outside light had ever seen these chambers and the flickering candle made the rough walls writhe as if alive. Phillipa gasped for breath in the foul air and thought this the closest thing she had ever seen to a grave.

With the accustomed ease of long practice, the housekeeper and scullery set to work. From various cupboards and crocks Mrs. Manning pulled and poured and sliced the viands, giving them to Florrie to stack on a rickety table. Phillipa found her mouth watering. All too aware of the weakness of the flesh, especially when the sin of gluttony was involved, Mrs. Manning's beady eyes never left her two minions, making sure that they snitched nothing from the table of their betters.

"Aye, that's it. We go now," she said, slamming and locking the cupboards with an unmistakable finality. Now Phillipa understood why Florrie always carried the loads; not because Mrs. Manning deemed herself too good to do so—which was doubtless true as well—but because she had to have her hands free to do the interminable locking-up. Every cupboard and every storeroom had its own lock and key and there was nothing that was not put away.

Phillipa took the loaded tray and followed in Mrs. Manning's wake through the absurdly narrow doorways and up the treacherously tilting stairs. As always, it was a revelation to watch the woman cook, taking less than promising comestibles and turning them into a passable meal. It made Phillipa wonder what she could do with decent victuals.

When at last all preparations were made, Mrs. Manning eyed Phillipa closely. "Listen, gel. I won't have any chit of a girl disgracing my kitchen. Tonight, Florrie will go with ye, but after that ye'll be on yer own and I don't want to hear any bad reports!" With a gesture of dismissal she waved her away and sat down heavily in her rocking chair.

Phillipa picked up the laden tray and gasped; the load was almost more than she could bear. How had Florrie, with her pitiful supply of strength, managed at all? Despite Phillipa's care and Florrie's aid, it was a painful trip upstairs, fraught with precariously balanced crockery, not to mention the almost unbearably enticing aroma of real food. Miss Stanhope-Fredericks had to exert a considerable amount of willpower to keep from flinging off the covers and gorging to her fill.

The first-floor parlor was reassuringly ordinary if not shabby; sorely faded red draperies masked the windows, looking as if they had not been opened in years. Phillipa could clearly perceive a spider's web strung in glittering profusion across half the width of one curtain.

In palmier days the carpet must have matched the curtains in hue, but now it took a concentrated search to find the original color between the vast stretches of pink canvas. Shabby, out-of-mode furniture such as decorated the attics of houses all over the country here was in general service, though grossly neglected; veneer warped and buckled, grime filled out the extremely ugly carving, pieces of hardware were inexplicably missing.

To Phillipa Stanhope-Fredericks, however, these impressions were all secondary to the expression in the eyes of a history master who made her very being vibrate. *How stupid,* she thought. *How incredibly stupid! I've had my pick of the ton, of the cream of English manhood, and the only man who has ever stirred me like this is a teacher in a suspicious boys' school!* She moaned inwardly, even as her pulse began to hammer.

Save for the one disconcerting glance from Geraint and an even more upsetting stare from Seth, none of the masters or monitors seemed to notice their presence. Florrie went right to work, nervous as a rabbit, murmuring to Phillipa in a barely audible undertone.

"Ah, is the pretty one going to serve us up here as well?" Seth's accent grated against Phillipa's nerves. "Delightful. You are awfully boring and not half so pretty."

"I do not see where that affects anything," Phillipa said impulsively, protecting Florrie just as in another world she had once protected Letty.

Panic filled Florrie's eyes. "Maggie! It was nothing. . . . Please."

Seth smiled and looked all the world like a small boy with a new pet to torment. "Aha! Our woman has spirit as well as beauty. Ye will provide an interesting . . . diversion." With another feral smile, the head monitor turned and walked back to his fellows.

Miss Stanhope-Fredericks shivered and felt as if she were in need of a bath. To think that such a creature was in a position of authority in a school that purported to be for young gentlemen. . . .

"Maggie, ye shouldn't have done that! He's a mean one to cross. . . ."

"He had no right to talk to you like that."

The thin shoulders shrugged. "Guess not, but words can't hurt me . . . they've said worse things. Maggie, please don't concern yerself fighting for me. Ye'll have enough to manage on yer own." She managed a travesty of a smile. "Now, take the top tablecloth from this pile here . . . we changes the cloth every three days."

As Miss Stanhope-Fredericks watched, Florrie shook out the cloth with expert hands and draped it over the scarred old table, then set about the china and cutlery with more speed than grace and at last placed the dishes of food in the center, where each could serve himself.

"Dinner is served, gentlemen," Florrie said, then turned and took both the tray and Phillipa from the room, only to be stopped halfway through the hall by a spasm of coughing.

"It's drafty here. Let's get you down by the fire. And you must go to bed early tonight."

"Promise me, Maggie . . . watch yerself. Don't anger the monitors."

"I promise, Florrie. I promise," Phillipa said carelessly.

Once in the kitchen they settled down with Mrs. Manning to their own poor supper of leftover gruel and hard bread, preceded by the housekeeper's indigestible prayers. Phillipa was no longer bothered by the meals as she had been in the beginning, for she had developed the trick of eating without tasting; unsatisfying for the palate, but at least the stomach was full. Under the housekeeper's baleful eye Phillipa sent Florrie to bed immediately after supper and, after earnest promises to do all the work herself, tackled the dishes.

"Think ye'll get something by putting on this show?" Mrs. Manning said, sneering, shifting her ponderous bulk and making the rocking chair squeak in protest.

"Show?"

"Such care and concern for the gel . . ."

"Florrie is sick and should have a doctor and some rest!"

The older woman rose with an effort, crossing the room to Phillipa's side, malodorous waves of malice flowing from her. "And who will pay for that? A doctor, indeed! She's lucky we don't turn her out." Without warning, her hamlike fist fell across Phillipa's cheek in a blow that made the young girl stagger.

Phillipa took her anger out on the dishes and finished in record time, just as the service bell jangled. To her relief, the first-floor parlor was empty and only one lamp burned. Phillipa tried to ignore the monstrous shadows cast by the looming drapes and furniture and concentrated on cleaning the wrecked remains of the meal; now was not the time to let overstrained nerves and an active imagination get the better of her. Placing the tray on the serving table, Miss Stanhope-Fredericks began to stack the dirty plates and found a secret hope dashed—not a crumb, not a scrap of the meal was left. Her stomach contracted around the hard, immovable lump of gruel. How could they have been so piggish when she was so hungry?

"Well, if it isn't our so-proper little scullery. So concerned about hurting the feelings of that little wretch. She ain't got any feelings, ye know, not like real people."

Phillipa began to tremble both with anger and fear. What unmerciful teasing Florrie must have suffered at Seth's hands! The door clicked softly shut behind him.

"Did you forget something, sir?"

"No. I came to see ye."

Phillipa swallowed heavily. "Me, sir?" To her horror his hand slid gently up her arm to rest on the nape of her neck, leaving a trail of duck bumps behind as if she had been touched by a snake. "Please don't, sir."

His eyes glittered in the dim light. "Come, gel. We'll have our little secret . . ."

Almost as if in answer to an unvoiced prayer, the door swung open and Geraint Catton stepped in, seemingly surprised to find the room occupied. He knew that his reading of the situation had been correct by the low growl of frustration in the head monitor's throat and the pathetically grateful expression in Maggie's eyes. Apparently, the history master thought, he had not been the only one disturbed by those astonishing eyes.

"Oh, sorry," he said, his voice light. "Seemed to have left my package of Lucifers somewhere and just can't grade papers without my pipe." For emphasis he lifted a beautifully carved meerschaum from his pocket and toyed with it absently. "Something so calming about blowing a cloud . . ."

While the scullery made good her escape, he quickly wandered about the room, seeking the elusive Lucifers and engaging the head monitor in civil conversation when he endeavored to follow the pretty maid from the room.

Never in Miss Stanhope-Fredericks's life did she think that Mrs. Manning and that noisome kitchen would be a welcome sight, but just then it was a haven. Here she was safe, for not even the hulking Seth dared tangle with Mrs. Manning. Oh, but if he did, what a scene it would be!

That night Phillipa finished the dishes with a smile on her face, the first that had been there in many, many days.

CHAPTER ELEVEN

Florrie's condition was worse the next morning, her thin face suffused with the flush of fever, the skin dry and taut like a skull. She lay there, moving only when she coughed, unable even to wipe the flecks of blood from her lips. Still she struggled to rise, muttering thickly of chores and at last reluctantly acquiescing to Phillipa's refusal.

Mechanically Miss Stanhope-Fredericks did the morning chores, actions that had never before intruded on her sheltered world save by their results, finishing just as the housekeeper entered.

"Good morning, Mrs. Manning."

"Where's the other one?"

"Florrie is very ill. She can't even get up from bed, so I left her there. She needs a doctor."

The older woman snorted. "A doctor! A doctor for the likes of her! Let her stay in bed, but ye does her work . . . all of it." With that abrupt dismissal of Florrie's health, she turned her attention to breakfast, muttering all the while about the ingratitude of wretches who had no more concern than to get themselves sick when there was work to be done.

As the meal progressed Mrs. Manning ranted on

half to herself that poor, ugly little Florrie would not rouse and enflame the darker feelings of man's nature, but that Maggie was formed by the Devil simply for the purpose of seducing young boys from the path of salvation. Finally, in ringing tones, the housekeeper declared that headmaster's order or no headmaster's order, she herself would serve this morning; that no sacrifice or defiance was too great to preserve the lads from such a demoralizing influence.

Half amused and half revolted, Phillipa was glad enough of the arrangement, for it kept her from the heart-tearing sight of the pathetic children. She utilized her liberty for a momentary escape into the relative peace of the kitchen garden.

"Good morning, Maggie."

Phillipa started, then felt the familiar charge go through her at the sight of the history master's admirable form. "Good morning."

"I thought you would be in the breakfast hall."

"Mrs. Manning is serving this morning. She said that I am a danger to the lads, that I entice their thoughts away from their studies. . . ."

Phillipa had spoken lightly, but to her surprise Geraint nodded gravely. "In that, at least, she is right. You can enflame a man . . . and you would be much better off away from here."

"But they are only children."

"Seth isn't."

"I must thank you for your timely intervention last night. . . ."

"I was glad to be of service," he said smoothly. "But what about tonight? And tomorrow? And the rest?"

"I shall just have to be careful and be sure that such a situation does not arise again."

"You are an unusual woman, Maggie, but you should look out for yourself and let that little wench fend for herself. I daresay she's done it for a number of years."

Conflicting emotions coursed through Phillipa: first, anger that the sufferings of another human being should be so ignored by someone merely by virtue of status and privilege, forgetting that until mere days ago her reactions would have been the same; and second, remorse that she had not thought of Florrie, lying upstairs on her sickbed, since that first clash with the housekeeper.

"Your face is as transparent as glass, child. Did what I say upset you so?" Despite his resolutions to the contrary, Geraint Catton found himself being more and more fascinated by the contradictions in this potentially exquisite creature. She was much more interesting than the women he had met during his time on the Peninsula, and far outshone those hothouse flowers he had known in London so long ago, almost like another life as well as another identity. Apparently Maggie could accept the horrors of this place without turning a hair, but speaking against a little kitchen slavey drained the blood from her cheeks.

"No, it's just that Florrie is so very sick . . . and I forgot all about her."

"No one put her in your charge, Maggie. You won't survive very long if you try to take care of the whole world."

For a moment Phillipa hated him, him and all his unfeeling kind. "She's not the whole world, she's just

87

one girl who was very kind to me . . . and now she's sick."

"How ill is the girl?"

"She couldn't rise from her—she couldn't rise this morning," Phillipa said, remembering at the last minute that her mother had told her one never said the word "bed" to a gentleman, as it was most improper, raising passions in the male against which a gently bred female was powerless. "She coughs a lot, but this morning there's even more blood than usual. She's very weak. . . . Indeed, I don't understand how she's been working as long as she has . . . but she says she has no other place to go. Oh, how can the world be such an awful place?"

Geraint was touched by the innocent plaintiveness in her cry. He longed to take her in his arms and tell her that it was all right, that he would make it all right, but his senses of duty and purpose, twin guiding stars for most of his life, dictated another course of action, confining him to a diffidence he did not feel. "It is awful, my dear; more so than you can dream. Would you consider help from me? I have an aunt in Bath—a most respectable lady. If there is not room for you in her establishment, I'm sure she could help you find a place . . . one where you will not be mistreated." The urge to touch her was too great; gently his fingers brushed the bruise along the strong cheekbone and she flinched. "Yes, I had noticed it."

He was tender, so kind, his dark eyes so soft, that Phillipa melted. It was all she could do to keep from flying into his arms and sobbing all over his slightly shabby coat.

"I appreciate your kind offer, but I cannot accept

it." Arnold's face swam before her eyes. "For reasons of my own I must stay here."

"Maggie . . ."

"But if you could, please, extend your kindness to Florrie . . . she is so ill."

"You say that she's coughing blood?"

"Yes, more than ever."

"Snodgress and Manning should be shot, letting the girl stay here," Geraint snarled, his face frighteningly grim.

"But she had no place to go."

"There are hospitals! Most of them have charity wards if the girl has no money. Don't you realize that other people can catch her illness? She shouldn't be allowed to prepare food, for the disease can be transmitted that way. Whole villages in the Peninsula have been wiped out by that stuff. . . . I hope your room is not too near hers . . ."

Phillipa could almost smile at thinking of their drafty floor as a room. "We share an attic. Could you please get her a doctor?"

"I will try—but stay away from her as much as possible, will you, Maggie? Believe me, that disease is a killer."

There was no answer to his request, much as Phillipa would have liked to have done anything he asked of her. Florrie had helped her when she had needed it and she could not in all honor refuse her. "I must go, Mr. Catton. Mrs. Manning will be needing me."

His fingers gently edged the bruise again. "She did this?"

"Yes. I angered her, though quite unintentionally."

"She is a brute."

There was no answer to his dispassionate observation, so Phillipa, more aroused by his casual kindness than by any number of passionate declarations given her in London, reentered the prison of a kitchen to begin preparations for the masters' breakfast.

Mr. Snodgress was angry; so was Mrs. Manning. They came into the kitchen together, bringing with them a charged cloud of vibrating emotion. Mrs. Manning spent so much of her time in blowing and bluster that the effect of her fury was blunted. Mr. Snodgress, however, being habitually calm and serene, was made the more terrible by his rage with white compressed lips and slitted eyes.

"You overstep yourself, woman."

"I work the ways of the Lord, Mr. Snodgress, and His ways come before all others. I must do what I see right."

"I gave you an order and I will not have it disobeyed."

The housekeeper waved a wild arm in Phillipa's direction. "That one is the Devil's work, sir. The boys should not be exposed to such a one. She will only—"

"I will decide the policy of the school, Mrs. Manning. Not you," the headmaster said in a voice that could cut paper. "After lunch you will come to my office and we will discuss this matter further."

Mrs. Manning waited until the baize door slammed behind him, then exhaled greatly, as if after a physical contest. Her keys jangled. "We'd best be getting the breakfast. It be getting late."

Phillipa was hard put not to laugh. Late, and the sun just now clearing the horizon.

Later, hesitating only a moment to consider the consequences, Phillipa placed the groaning tray of food for the masters' breakfast on the landing and wrapped two biscuits and a piece of pork sausage in a napkin, stuffing the package into her pocket. If she were going to regain her strength, Florrie had to eat more than the poor gruel that would be their breakfast.

Two bowls of that same gruel were waiting on the table when Phillipa returned. Mrs. Manning motioned for her to sit.

"I'll just take Florrie's up first—she must be hungry."

The older woman looked up balefully. "No one gets meals taken to them here. If she be hungry, let her come down."

"But she's sick. She can't come down."

"Then she don't eat," Mrs. Manning snapped. "If we let her get away with this little act, the whole school would be playing sick and wanting us to wait on them. She'll come down to work when she gets hungry enough. I warned Mr. Snodgress about lack of proper discipline. Spare the rod and spoil the child, the Good Book says."

Horrified, Phillipa slid into her place and automatically reached for the spoon, only to recoil in pain as the housekeeper dealt her hand a smart slap.

"I don't know where ye was raised, lass, but in this house ye show respect for the Lord! Now fold yer hands like a proper Christian woman and bow yer head to Him."

At last the housekeeper finished, though her sanctimonious, perverted rambling had taken so long that they had to bolt their cold gruel in order to clear the plates from the dining hall on time. Mrs. Manning took on that duty herself, giving Phillipa the few precious moments needed to sprint up to the attic and press the food parcel into Florrie's hands.

"Here, eat, but don't let Mrs. Manning know."

The fever-bright eyes filled with tears. "Ye stole this from the masters' table. . . . ye'll be sent to the punishment box if they find out—that's where she died. . . . Take care, Maggie . . ."

"They won't find out if you don't tell." As quickly as she had come, Phillipa hurried down the stairs and was pumping water into the heating cauldron as Mrs. Manning entered, laden with dirty dishes.

"Lazy creature! That water should have been near the boil now." The imperious sound of the front bell interrupted her tirade, and she contented herself with a frown. "Well, don't let it be ringing again! Ah, good-fer-nothing gels . . . keeping the gentry waiting . . ."

Doubtless Mrs. Manning would call Mr. Dinsworthy one of the gentry, so her prediction was essentially correct. The absurd creature minced into the hall, not bothering to remove his extremely dusty hat, and favored Miss Stanhope-Fredericks with a leer.

"Ye are much faster today. Tell Mr. Snodgress that I am here," he piped, the shrill voice carrying a sneer which belied the pink dimples of his face.

"Yes, sir," Phillipa said, remembering at the last moment to curtsy. Mr. Dinsworthy! She had entirely forgotten Mr. Dinsworthy. What part did he play in this?

The masters were still at breakfast. The odor of sausage and eggs made Phillipa's head reel. In her stomach the gruel lay as immovable as earth.

Mr. Snodgress's temper had not been improved by a good meal. "Well, girl, what is it? We didn't ring."

"Your pardon, sir, but Mr. Dinsworthy is downstairs, and he requested that you be told."

Something most strange then happened, incomprehensible to Phillipa, for a single glance skipped from man to man, charging the heavy air of the room with anticipation, as before a summer storm. Mr. Snodgress rose, dabbing at his lips with a dirty napkin.

"Very well, girl. The gentlemen here will ring when they're ready. I'll see Mr. Dinsworthy."

Other than the arrival of the funny little tradesman, the hours passed without untoward incident and to her surprise Phillipa found that it was midafternoon. How easy it was to become a working machine, a thing with neither mind nor soul, merely living from one moment to the next. Depleted in mind and body, Miss Stanhope-Fredericks stepped outside and sat on the kitchen curb, wrapped in despair. How many days, how many lifetimes had she spent and suffered here and how little she had learned! Had she not been so exhausted, she could have wept.

"Don't make so much noise! They'll hear!" came a hoarse whisper from behind her back, followed by a violent shushing and a rustling of foliage.

With a hoydenish action that would have caused her dear mother to faint, Phillipa swung her legs over the low wall and dropped to earth not an arm's distance from them.

Two little faces looked up into hers, each with the seal of doom written on it. Phillipa thought that such a look should have been seen only on the face of a convicted felon, never a schoolboy.

"Now, who are you?" she asked through rising tears. They were both so young and so reminiscent of Arnold, in their maroon and gray uniforms. They looked at each other, scared, panicky glances, as if gauging their chances for escape. "Come, now! I won't hurt you."

Chunky and strangely adult for one so young, the bigger boy cleared his throat. "Who are you?"

"I'm the scullery. They call me Maggie."

"You don't look like a scullery."

"I'm not normally," Miss Phillipa Stanhope-Fredericks answered with perfect truth. "Who are you?"

"I'm Ian Gorman. This is Walter Hastings. He's only first form."

"Why do you look so scared?"

"We aren't supposed to be in the garden. Are you going to tell on us?"

"What would happen if I did?"

"They would punish us."

"If you know you aren't supposed to be here, why are you?"

Another quick look passed before Ian spoke. "We're hungry."

Only with a strong effort did Phillipa keep from gathering the pair of them in her arms and weeping. To think of a school that let boys get so hungry that the half-grown vegetables in a kitchen garden were tempting enough to risk punishment to steal. At that moment Miss Stanhope-Fredericks was capable of murder.

Instead, she spoke, but with a decidedly unsteady voice. "I'm sorry . . . I'm hungry too. Boys . . . will you answer some questions if I promise not to tell anyone that I saw you here?"

94

"Why should we trust you?" Ian asked with a heart-breakingly adult cynicism.

"Why should I trust you?" Phillipa countered. "Remember, I can be sent to the punishment box too."

It was the blind mention of the punishment box that made the two small heads nod. "All right," Ian said.

"How long have you been here?"

"I've been here three years," Ian calculated, using his fingers. "This is Walter's first year."

"Why do your parents send you back to this awful place? Can't you tell them how bad it is here? Won't they believe you?"

Another look flew between the boys. "We don't have any parents," Walter piped up.

"Almost none of the boys do. Mr. Snodgress prefers it that way," Ian sneered. "He says most guardians don't care enough to meddle like parents would. I heard him say it to one of the monitors after they thought we were asleep. My guardian didn't want to be bothered with me after my parents died, so he sent me here. That's the way it is with most of us. There's only a few boys whose fathers are old boys. Living ones, that is." His voice was bitter. "Mr. Snodgress keeps the place open all year round, even during the holidays, so no one is forced to deal with us."

Walter spoke again. His childish treble was slightly higher than Ian's. "My uncle says it costs an absolute fortune to keep me here, but it's worth it to get me off his hands."

"Dear Heaven! Did he say such a thing to your face?"

"No, it was to my aunt. They thought I was outside." The pudgy face was stoic and immobile.

"You poor children. . . . If your guardians are paying so much money, why is so little of it being spent on you?"

They were silent. "I don't know," Ian said finally.

"And who is Mr. Dinsworthy?"

"I think he owns an inn at Canton-on-Marley. The Boar's Head. It's south of here, five miles or so."

"That's right," Walter said. "My uncle and I stayed there on the way here. There was the most delicious food . . ."

"Boys, I've got to go now or the cook will be awfully angry with me." Phillipa swung back over the low wall, her mind working at furious speed. She had so much information and none of it made any sense; so far nothing made any sense and she was no closer to the reason for Arnold's death. It was most depressing.

The rest of the evening passed amazingly quickly; even Phillipa, from her limited vantage point, could sense an uneasy feeling of expectancy permeating the school, a sense of something waiting to be fulfilled. Not even Mrs. Manning was immune to the strange atmosphere, for she was more snappish than usual, barking out orders and watching over her shoulder as if expecting a visit from the Avenging Angel. Then, after their poor supper of bread and cheese and the completion of the dishes, a most unimaginable thing happened.

Leaning over the hob for the boiling kettle, Mrs. Manning spoke almost kindly. "Gel . . . Maggie . . . perhaps I misjudged ye. Ye've done the work of three today and nary a word of complaint. Sit ye down here."

Stunned, Phillipa sank into the hard wooden chair and watched as the housekeeper prepared tea in an old earthenware pot.

"I thought ye'd like a cup of tea."

Phillipa's mouth watered. "Yes, please."

It made no difference that the tea was cheap enough to float like dust on the top of the cup and was heart-stoppingly strong. It was tea, and the first she had tasted in days and days. She sipped the cup slowly, making it last, savoring the warmth. Unaccustomed to the leisure, the heat from the fire and the tea, she was unable to restrain a series of utterly satisfying yawns.

"Yuv been a good gel, Maggie. Get ye to bed."

Reeling with fatigue, Phillipa bade the older woman a civil good night and staggered up to the attic, not even noticing the dark, but still conscious enough to feel a kind of guilt that Florrie had not crossed her mind in hours. Phillipa tried to ignore her companion's labored breathing and salved her conscience by promising to do something about getting her a doctor the next day, no matter what had to be done.

Too tired even to remove her grimy dress, Miss Stanhope-Fredericks fell across the thin mattress, glad that none of her family or Letty could see her now. What a blessing each of them thought her somewhere else, for as complicated as this problem was getting, there was no way she could even begin to explain things now. With the aid of Fate, however, Phillipa thought, things would work out all right.

CHAPTER TWELVE

Unbeknownst to Miss Stanhope-Fredericks, Fate had already taken a hand in her affairs, in the unlikely guise of Lady Lettice Winterthorpe. For perhaps the thousandth time she read the letter that her dear Phillipa had sent the day before.

Dearest Letty—

What an unpleasantness for you. I know all too well the sinister aspect of His Grace of Lowood—who is a nobleman only in lineage, not in aspect or behavior—and sympathize most deeply with you. At this time I am unable to do aught to help you—if under any circumstances at all I could—beyond offering you my love, my support, and my courage. I beg you not to accept the fate of being Duchess of Lowood just yet. Surely there is some way to resolve the question of your future. Be of good faith, Letty, and think of me as—

Your affectionate
Phillipa

Letty frowned; the letter was so general, so abstract, so unlike the dauntless Phillipa she knew. Of course, Phillipa was staying with her old nurse, Kirky, and Kirky's sister, who by all accounts was a Tartar. Under such auspices she could hardly have written a letter of insurrection, however much she wanted to. According to what Phillipa had told her of Mrs. Selkirk, dear Kirky's formidable sister, she would be all too capable of censoring Phillipa's correspondence.

Of course! It was a coded message; something was there that she had to look beneath the surface to find. The stablehand had said, in the short half-minute they had conversed, that Miss Stanhope-Fredericks had written the note quickly—indeed, the handwriting was agitated, as if done at great speed. There would have been no time to work out an elaborate code, so it had to be the content that Phillipa had used to carry her message. Oh, if only she weren't so slow of wit, Letty mourned, she could have divined what her dear friend meant without all this trouble.

"Lettice?"

Letty barely had time to shove the much-read missive under the pillow before her mother entered the room. Eustacia looked her best these days, filled with a life and energy that would not have shamed a woman fifteen years her junior.

"Lettice, this will not do! Your face is all swollen."

"I have been crying, Mamma."

"So I see. What a foolish girl you are. Well, cucumber slices and then some Lotion of the Ladies of Denmark will take care of that. We can't have you looking like such a fright."

"I'm sorry, Mamma."

"Now, His Grace of Lowood is going to call this afternoon to make his formal offer to you, and I do hope you comport yourself more like a lady than last time. I was positively mortified at your behavior. How could you embarrass me so? It would have served you right if he had changed his intentions, but luckily I was able to convince him that you were merely overcome by the honor he planned to bestow on you." Eustacia smiled a lovely smile that made those who knew her intimately shudder with apprehension. "You will behave like a lady this afternoon?"

"I have the headache, Mamma."

Eustacia stamped her foot. Really, what had she done to be saddled with such a ninnyhammer, and such a plain-looking one at that, for her only child? "Well, you can say yes to His Grace very prettily, even with a headache, and then you can come upstairs. I do not understand you, child! You have no conversation, only a passable face, and you turn up your nose when I arrange the most advantageous marriage available in the country!"

"I do not love His Grace, Mamma. He frightens me."

"Love!" the duchess shrieked. "What has love to do with it? Do you think I loved your father? Only peasants marry for love—it's nothing more than humors in the blood anyway. You are the daughter of a duke, Lettice, and you will be a duchess in your own right, with jewels and houses and carriages and horses . . . all that anyone could desire!" With a brilliant mastery of herself, the Duchess of Connaught caught her breath and then spoke in a very gentle, controlled tone. "You will greet His Grace cordially and accept his offer with pleasure. I will not let you ruin my plans." Only the slam of the door behind her betrayed her agitation.

Shaking as she always did after even the mildest confrontation with her mother, Lettice took the letter from under her pillow and searched fervently for the hidden message that she now felt sure Phillipa had sent her. *"I am unable to do aught to help you"—that must mean that she is unable to come herself,* Letty thought—*"beyond offering you my love, my support, and my courage. Surely there is some way to resolve the question . . ."*

Some way to resolve the question . . . love, support . . . courage. . . . Phillipa would have to send her lots of courage, thought Letty, sighing, for who knew better that she had none of her own? That was it! Phillipa was telling her to act as she would in the circumstances . . . *My love, my support, my courage.* Phillipa must mean that Letty must run away from Connaught House and join her. Of course, if she were found out, it would ruin her forever, but she could face that with equanimity compared to marrying the Duke of Lowood and having his dry hands and cold eyes on her. . . .

From Ivy Cottage she could appeal to her father; since the hunting accident that had left him an invalid he had not left Coombs Farm, but surely he could not let his only daughter be forced into a distasteful alliance. The risk was appalling, Letty realized, but the surety of the duke's call that afternoon was worse, and so it was that when Jennings came to announce the Duke of Lowood to his young mistress, he found the

101

room empty, with no trace of Lady Lettice nor a clue to where she had gone.

If Letty had been hoping for a joyous, congratulatory reunion with Phillipa at the end of her long ride, on which she was accompanied only by her friend the stableman, her hopes were doomed to disappointment. After rousing the entire household at Ivy Cottage, she was told not only that Phillipa was not there, but that she was not herself, for Miss Stanhope-Fredericks was even now with Lady Lettice and her father at Coombs Farm. Only after a long and protracted argument, during which Letty broke into well-deserved tears of exhaustion and was comforted by Kirky, was the stableman moved to speak, stating unequivocally that the young lady was indeed Lady Lettice Winterthorpe.

To Mrs. Amanda Selkirk, servants were like furniture: one only noticed them when something was wrong or missing. This young person, however, was vaguely familiar and it was only a moment before Mrs. Selkirk had him pegged as the man who had brought the note to Phillipa. Despite his natural reticence in the presence of one so imposing as the elder Selkirk sister and his vow to Miss Stanhope-Fredericks for silence, he was ultimately encouraged to tell everything that was in his power. The reactions to his revelations were varied: Letty was overawed at the courage of her friend to play so bold a game; Kirky was distraught with worry over the thousands of horrors that could at this moment be befalling her nursling; and Mrs. Selkirk was satisfied and secure in the knowledge that her theories about Miss Stanhope-Fredericks being a wild, fast chit were so amply proved. It was, she repeated again and again with emphasis, obviously an elopement. Kirky and Letty, made allies by both their affection for Phillipa and their awe of Amanda Selkirk, simultaneously cried nay, that it must be some pressing and important matter on which Phillipa wished to spare them worry, or that she had been most foully abducted by villains. They were equally divided on the cause, until Mrs. Selkirk interjected with some asperity that she felt sorry for any villain unlucky enough to cross that saucy baggage's path.

The thought of her darling charge in the hands of brigands or lechers quite naturally brought Kirky to the edge of an hysterical spasm, and with Letty's inexpert but well-meaning help and the attitude of Mrs. Selkirk—whom Lady Lettice roundly apostrophized as an unfeeling monster and a discredit to her sex, before she herself burst into tears once more—it was some time before any sensible suggestions could be made.

After a flash of inspiration on Kirky's part, the stablehand—who would just as soon have been away from such a violent scene—was dispatched to fetch Mr. Stanhope-Fredericks, bearing with him all of their hopes that Miss Stanhope-Fredericks would be found to have been with her mother since leaving the protection of Ivy Cottage.

Fortunately, Mrs. Stanhope-Fredericks was enjoying a rather good turn of health and Mr. Stanhope-Fredericks, carefully concealing from her his mission and intent, was able to leave her, making it to Ivy Cottage a little after tea the following day, having run at least three changes of prime stock into the ground.

Once arrived, the lateness of the hour did not deter him. After a detailed conversation with the three ladies—two tearful and one indignant—he set about dispatching discreetly worded notes to the coaching inn and to Worthington Grange. Letty and Kirky alternately lamented about the probable fate of their beloved Phillipa, which in their fevered imaginings ranged from being kidnapped by brigands while rushing to the side of her mother to being spirited away by an importunate lover unwilling or unable to win her hand through conventional channels. Mrs. Selkirk called them both ninnies and Miss Stanhope-Fredericks a regrettable hoyden, then proceeded to take Mr. Stanhope-Fredericks to task about the lamentable upbringing his daughter had received.

Augustus Stanhope-Fredericks had met Amanda Selkirk on a few occasions and disliked her intensely, but had borne her company out of affection and consideration for Kirky. Now, however, partly out of sheer honesty and partly as a way of releasing his tightly strung emotions, he rounded on Mrs. Selkirk with a forceful rebuttal that soon reduced her to a state which in a lesser woman might be called weeping.

Within twenty-four hours he had answers to both his inquiries. The estimable Fanchon wrote at length, describing the unease he had felt when the young person named Maggie had shown up at the Grange unannounced, bearing Miss Phillipa's clothing and a note that sounded quite unlike that estimable young lady. But being trained to serve well no matter the oddity of the orders put before him, Fanchon had followed the miss's instructions without question. The young person Maggie was an acceptable sort and her presence in the servants' hall had not been disruptive, save when two of the grooms had disagreed about who thought her eyes were prettiest, but he, Fanchon, had quickly put a period to such nonsense. On receiving Mr. Stanhope-Frederick's missive, however. Fanchon had had what he termed a conversation with the wench, and had brought forth the information that he was gratified to be able to send on. Fanchon quite rightly felt a pride in the job he had done, getting the information about Miss Phillipa's intent to bring the scoundrels responsible for her brother's death to book, but pragmatic being that he was, he had not allowed for the heroism of spirit that lurks in the hearts of the romantically inclined.

Maggie, true to the spirit of the young miss's quest, had told the formidable Fanchon the truth, but only a part. She had kept to herself Miss Phillipa's plan of becoming a chambermaid, harboring somewhere in her mind the idea of running away herself to St. Gregory's in order to warn Miss Stanhope-Fredericks of the approaching interference and thereby not only saving the idol of her childish daydreams but garnering a little of the glory for herself. Unfortunately, however, after her enforced confession to the butler, she was suddenly regarded as an untrustworthy person and, while not precisely incarcerated, she was certainly watched, which ruined any heroic plans she might have had.

Mr. Stanhope-Fredericks was not surprised at the contents of his replies; knowing Phillipa's affection for poor Arnold and her impulsive, courageous nature, and beginning to fear a criminal lack of discretion regarding Sir Percy Hightower's—Cubby's—letter, the idea that his daughter might attempt something of the sort was not unbelievable. At least now he knew the area in which to search for her, but how, without ruining her entirely, could he find her and pull her through this scrape? He would start out in the morning, but his own movements would be made with caution, so as not to upset any plans Hightower might currently have in motion.

At that moment, far away and in another world, Lord Ronald Mickleham boarded a boat barely in time to catch the evening tide. Having just been granted a long overdue leave, he was looking forward to a relaxing, leisurely holiday in England with his friends and loved ones.

CHAPTER THIRTEEN

In the morning Florrie had no need for a doctor. They found her at the foot of the main stairway, her neck broken and grotesquely twisted. She was in her night rail and barefooted on the cold floor, unwarmed by as little as a shawl.

Miss Stanhope-Fredericks awoke slowly, lying fully clothed on her filthy mattress, her mouth tasting as if it had been stuffed with foul cotton wool, her limbs dead weights. She noticed Florrie's empty bed and hurried downstairs, trying to decide whether to chide her for arising so soon from a sickbed or to thank her for the extra sleep.

Alarmed by the empty kitchen, she began to explore toward the front of the house, finally reaching the front hall, where a grim-faced knot of people were clustered about the stairs.

A strong hand gripped her elbow authoritatively, effectively stopping her progress, and she looked up into the history master's set face. "Don't look, Maggie."

"What's happened?"

Mrs. Manning turned to look at her with red-rimmed eyes. "Aye, the poor gel . . . she was a good lass, was Florrie. . . ."

"Florrie!" Phillipa cried and lunged for the horrid, still object on the floor, now mercifully covered, but was held immobile by Geraint's restraining hand.

"The girl broke her neck, Maggie," Geraint said in answer to Phillipa's mute inquiry. "There's nothing to be done."

"Dead?" Phillipa murmured, fighting back waves of horror and nausea. The foul taste of that dead sleep was still with her and it grew to miasmic proportions.

Seth detached himself from the others and stared with contemptuous disdain at the mourning servants. "Enough of that. Ye'd best be about yer morning chores. There be the living to attend to."

"He's right, Maggie," Mrs. Manning said, her voice still unfamiliarly gentle. "Breakfast is near an hour late."

For a moment Geraint's fingers tightened over her

wrist as if he would detain her, but then they relaxed and he walked to join the sad group at the foot of the stairs. The object on the floor was horridly, unnaturally still. It was so hard to believe that it was Florrie under that blanket. Florrie, so quick, so uncomplaining. . . .

The mysterious officialities of death occupied the front of the house most of the day. The magistrate had come to investigate and make a judgment on Florrie's passing. Mr. Snodgress himself came to the kitchen when it was Maggie's turn to testify.

"Girl, the squire wishes to talk to you. Now, be a good girl and tell the truth without any sass." The words were curiously gentle, but the expression in his eyes conveyed a definite threat. Meekly Phillipa followed him back to the front parlor, debating the wisdom of telling this justice the little she knew and the volumes she suspicioned.

The first sight of Squire Mullavey disabused Miss Stanhope-Fredericks of any notion of being anything but a stupid serving girl. An extremely aged man, the squire was also exceedingly fat, the great bulk of his stomach so large, he could not see his knees. A Ramilles wig such as had gone out of style twenty years before was perched at a precarious angle on his seemingly bald head, and two dull, lackluster eyes peered from the great flabby face.

"Well, gel, come here, come here. I'll speak to this one alone, Snodgress, alone."

Mr. Snodgress made an obsequious bow, and with a telling look at Phillipa, departed, no doubt to just outside the door, where all would be audible. Phillipa bobbed a curtsy to the justice as courtesy demanded. He did not offer her a seat.

"What's yer name, gel, yer name?"

"I be called Maggie, sir."

"Tell me all ye know . . . all ye know."

There was no way to confide in this man. With a mental apology to Florrie, Phillipa recited just what Mr. Snodgress would have wanted to hear. "She was sick, sir, coughing and running a fever. She was raving a bit yesterday and unable to get up. I tried to do both of our tasks. . . . I slept soundly last night and didn't hear her get up."

"Ah, that confirms what I've heard . . . confirms it. The gel must have been delirious! Yes, that's it, delirious. Snodgress!"

The headmaster must have had his ear to the panels, for he almost fell into the room. "Yes, Squire?"

"That's all I need to know. Sick gel—delirium—accidental death. Bad business having a sick gel here at the school, Snodgress, bad business." With a snort that would have done justice to an elephant, he blew his nose into an exceedingly capacious handkerchief.

"I know, sir," Snodgress said smoothly, "but we just couldn't turn the child out for a short illness. It came on her so suddenly, poor creature. . . ."

Phillipa dug her nails painfully into her palms until the skin broke, struggling for self-control. How could Snodgress be such a liar and everyone believe him?

The squire stood, his ripples of fat rearranging themselves with wavelike motions. "I think that will be all we need, Snodgress . . . all we need. Death by misadventure. No need for a fuss, no need at all."

"Please, sir," Phillipa said, and both men looked surprised; her presence had been forgotten.

"Yes, gel?"

"When will the services be? I'd like to go if I may, sir."

The squire looked at Phillipa almost kindly. He was probably very sweet to his grandchildren, she thought. "Gel, she's already been taken away. It's over."

"But it was only this morning."

"She had no family—no one. There was no need to wait. She was buried this morning at the charity grounds. Yes, no need to wait."

Phillipa's dismay was plain. "But without a service?"

"The workhouse parson read the words over her . . . all the words. . . ." The squire's tone implied that such a being as Florrie could have expected no more. Phillipa could have wept. Such speed just wasn't decent.

Snodgress frowned with displeasure. "Don't be bothering the squire, girl."

"No bother, no bother at all. Pretty little thing, ain't she?"

"We consider Maggie quite an addition to the school, Squire Mullavey. Would you care for some tea or perhaps something a little stronger?"

The squire looked thirsty for a moment, licking his lips, then shook his head. In the normal way he was never averse to a bit of refreshment, but today was just too exciting. Never in all his years of being squire of the district had he had so many important duties at once. It was about time everyone became aware of his talents and his worth. "No, thank you, no. Must run along and see a gentleman . . . very interesting case, very interesting. I'm sworn to secrecy, of course, regarding the gentleman's identity, but it seems his daughter disappeared in this neighborhood. Seems to think brigands abducted her or some such nonsense, as if such a thing could happen in this area. In this neighborhood! Gel's something of a high-flyer, I gather, a real high-flyer—probably run off with someone. . . ." He laughed until his eyes were wet. "Father's always the last to know, don't you know, always the last to know. Still, must go through the proper form. . . ."

Miss Stanhope-Fredericks was intensely glad that the headmaster's attention was focused on the squire's departure, for surely one glance at her face would reveal her secret. Perhaps he had already guessed and was coming back to denounce her. . . . The gentleman in question, of course, could only be her own father. How had they found out she was missing? How did he know to come looking for her here? That stupid Maggie—the real one—must have talked, of course; it was the only thing that made sense. Drat the girl! Phillipa's mouth set into a grim line. This complication only meant that she had to move fast.

Suddenly it was midafternoon and Phillipa was free for a while, a time graciously granted by the housekeeper so that she could pray for the soul of the "dear departed" while Mrs. Manning conferred with Mr. Snodgrass.

Phillipa's heart convulsed with bitterness. *A little more concern lavished on Florrie's body while alive and a little less on her soul after death might have made all the difference,* Phillipa thought. Odd, but since she had come to this place she had been a very light sleeper, so much so that it would have been most unusual for Florrie to be able to get up and go downstairs without awakening her. And what had she been doing on the front steps? Phillipa sat on the secluded bower bench in the desolate rose garden, helpless tears trickling from her eyes.

"It doesn't make any sense, does it?"

Phillipa looked up into the history master's dark eyes and was comforted by his presence. It would be so tempting to fling herself against him, to cry out all her problems and griefs onto his strong shoulders. . . . "No. She was such a good girl at heart and they wouldn't even hold a service for her, not a proper one . . . just some words at the charity grounds. It isn't right."

Geraint felt his heart touched by her distress. "No, it isn't right," he murmured, sitting next to her and fighting the impulse to hold her close, to protect her against whatever threatened. Strange that his heart, hardened by many years of exposure to the female sex in its infinite variety, should be so affected by a pair of steady blue eyes awash with slow tears.

"She should have seen a doctor. Mrs. Manning wouldn't even let me take meals up to her." Gratefully Phillipa accepted his proffered handkerchief, noting that it was made of exquisitely fine linen.

"That woman is utterly heartless." He cleared his throat and looked at the spring sky. "Maggie, won't you reconsider my offer? My aunt in Bath . . . This isn't a fitting place for you."

"Thank you, Mr. Catton, but I can't leave just yet. Please don't ask."

112

"Very well, I won't, but please remember . . ." His hand clasped around hers and they stared deeply into each other's eyes. Around them the burgeoning rose-buds swam in scent, but neither noticed. "The offer still stands. I should like to help you."

There was a moment of silence more eloquent than words, then he rose abruptly to stalk from the garden. Miss Stanhope-Fredericks was hard put not to call the man with the strong shoulders back.

CHAPTER FOURTEEN

It seemed as if the house would never settle down. On the other side of the thin partition Mrs. Manning slept fitfully, low moans breaking her snores, punctuated with the protesting squeals of the bed as she heaved from side to side. Phillipa lay taut and wakeful in the dark, halfway convinced of all the wild tales of haunts Florrie had told her.

Finally, when even the great banked fire had ceased to pop and settle, Phillipa rose from her sleepless pallet and, guided only by courage and instinct, felt her way quietly through the breathing dark to Mr. Snodgress's office. No thread of light showed from any door, yet by now it would have seemed that the mere thudding of her heart alone would have roused the house.

No sound, save that of her own labored breath, disturbed the velvet blackness. Her old fear of the dark temporarily subdued, Phillipa closed the door and crept across to the desk. Finding the wasted stump of a candle, her searching fingers then felt in her apron pocket for the tinderbox pilfered from the kitchen.

Strangely enough, the pale light was more frightening than the dark. Her eyes dulled by fatigue, Phillipa watched as the furniture took on strange forms and writhed menacingly with the candle's flickering; evil gleams winked back from the tarnished brasses, almost as if from eyes. Still, Phillipa reminded herself resolutely, light was necessary to her purpose and, ignoring the activity around her (surely those draperies weren't *breathing*!), she applied herself to the desk.

In his supreme arrogance, Mr. Snodgress had not even bothered to lock the drawers, which was a blessing, and Phillipa pulled forth a fat, official-looking ledger. In neat columns inside were the names and records of all students in the recent history of St. Gregory's. Biting her lip for control, Miss Stanhope-Fredericks skimmed down the page until she found: Stanhope-Fredericks, Arnold. Date of departure. Reason for departure . . . died.

There. No reason, no explanation, just "died." For one unbelievable moment Phillipa was swamped in despair. She had risked everything, been found out by her family and who knew else, suffered as she never had before, and for what? The hope that in the private records of the school there would be something more substantial than just "died."

With an effort she came back to the present, ready to fight again. The candle was burning lower and there was still much to be done. Replacing the ledger, she systematically ransacked the next drawer, taking care not to disturb the contents, as the headmaster was a meticulous housekeeper. There were itemized envelopes of receipts from the butcher, the greengrocer, the coal chandler, each dated and signed for enormous amounts. Phillipa read on with a growing sense of bewilderment. Where had all of this gone? There had been no evidence of six large mutton roasts, or of five hundredweight of heating coal. Where were the bags of choice potatoes and the cheddar wheels? It was a mystery.

The next drawer was devoted to stationery, entirely, it would seem, for the drawer was brimming full; strange that a rural master of a small school would require so much in the way of writing supplies. The next and last drawer contained nothing but extremely ill-written pages that were instantly recognizable as student assignments.

Nothing! Bitterness rose in her throat as palpable as ashes. Could there be another hiding place for this shadowy, indefinable proof for which she was searching? Her eyes raked the room, but it still seemed most logical that if there were anything to be hidden, a man would hide it in his desk, the most obvious and therefore the safest place, if he concealed it cleverly. Hurrying now, for the candle was making tiny wet dying sounds, Phillipa went through the desk again, cautiously feeling beneath the top layers.

There—in the strangely full stationery drawer—her probing fingers found something. There were hard edges—A box? A book?—beneath the papers. Her heart beat rapidly, almost suffocating her with fear and anticipation. . . . So close, so close . . .

Abruptly the candle gave a last, dying glare and the darkness swooped down in tactile suffocation. Phillipa's tongue was dry and filled her mouth, tasting like a stale rag. Every nursery horror that had ever plagued her came back with a full load of terror. Surely no wind could make that mournful noise, no night animal that cry! Panic was pushing, crowding, beating at the doors of her mind, trying to take over. . . .

Oddly enough, it was a sound that should have been more frightening than all imaginary terrors put together that snapped Phillipa from her paralysis: Outside in the hallway an incautious footstep brought a heel into unintentionally noisy contact with flooring, making a sound like a drum. Someone was coming.

With the speed of a hunted animal, Phillipa slid the drawer closed and searched the dark room with her mind, probing for a hiding place. The drapes! It was chilly behind the red velvet hangings, with no barrier between her back and the drafts that danced through the casement, and the dust was thick enough to choke anyone foolish enough to breathe deeply. Miss Stanhope-Fredericks fastidiously tried not to think about spiders and cobwebs and black beetles, concentrating instead on staying far enough back so that her shoetips would not show beneath the fabric, betraying her presence.

A soft glow filled the room, far brighter than her poor candle had ever been. Behind the drapes the red in the room seemed to glow, casting an eerie light.

Phillipa found that by cautiously shifting her position she could peep through one of the innumerable moth holes to get a fair view of the room.

Geraint Catton sat at the desk, his fine profile sharply outlined by the brace of candles, gently riffling through the drawers as she had done only moments before. Fatigue and strain were making Phillipa fanciful. She wondered, *If objects could think, how would that desk react to two such violations in one night?*

Unaware of being observed, Geraint sat back from his superficial search and pondered, his noble brow disfigured by a frown. Unconsciously his hand massaged his wounded leg; the damp and cold bothered it so. Several minutes later he finally rose and left, apparently having accepted the contents of the desk just as he saw it. Phillipa stayed behind the curtains for a good half hour, despite bone-deep weariness and the lack of light. The idea of finding another candle and continuing her own search was unenticing, and even her fear of the dark was pushed into second place by a new line of thought: What was Geraint Catton's involvement in this place? What was he looking for? And why?

The day was dragging on. Phillipa, stupid with fatigue and lack of sleep, stumbled through her chores, earning more than one sharp reproof from the housekeeper. *Doubtless,* Phillipa thought, *after I am dead she will call me a "good gel" and cry long lamentations for my departed soul.* She did not even have the energy to weep.

Mrs. Manning, her temper shorter than usual, ordered Phillipa to be quick about picking some early berries. The plants had matured early in a sheltered part of the far garden and would provide a tasty treat for the masters' dinner.

Phillipa walked from the house, her mood lightened just by being outside. Also there was that curious mound at the edge of the garden, quite near the berry patch. It had seemed an oddity before and now it was even more so. Seen from a closer vantage, it did not seem large enough to be a funerary mound and apparently there had never been any sort of structure on it in the form of a folly or scenic ruin. In theory it could have been a root cellar, but why should anyone have bothered with one so far from the main kitchen when there existed that rabbit warren of storage under the kitchen?

Mindful of the housekeeper's admonition to hurry, Phillipa knelt as comfortably as possible amid the tangled berry plants. She began to pull at the fruit, putting almost as many into her hungry mouth as into the chipped earthenware bowl.

"Maggie!" Eerily, the voice seemed to come from both everywhere and nowhere.

Phillipa straightened. The hairs at the nape of her neck seemed to rise of their own volition; her heart began to beat an uncertain staccato of fear. Unnoticed, the berries she held were crushed to a pulp, staining her fingers with a color like blood.

"Please, Maggie, down here." The voice came again, hollow and distant, but it was—or had been—the voice of a boy.

Phillipa turned slowly, half expecting to see the shade of a beloved boy clad in maroon and gray. Instead she saw a white hand, tiny and grasping, seemingly reaching up from the ground itself. She was paralyzed, unable to scream. This couldn't actually exist, this couldn't really be! There were no such things as hands from the grave. . . .

No, of course there weren't! Phillipa's native common sense broke her fear and she knelt on the ground, seeing for the first time the small grating set in the hard-packed earth. The hand slid back through the bars and Phillipa peered down into the gloom, half expecting a window into Hades. In a way it was, for the room beneath the sod was small, scarcely bigger than a stair landing and extremely low. The boy could not stand upright. The walls and floor of beaten earth were shiny with moisture and there was an unhealthy smell of mold and damp.

"Oh, Maggie, I'm ever so glad you came."

"Ian! What are you doing here? What is this?"

The tiny face crumpled quizzically. "I thought you knew . . . this is the punishment box."

Miss Stanhope-Fredericks's mouth formed a large *O*. This was where the "bad boys" were sent; this was the hellhole that had only been hinted at.

"I'm so hungry, Maggie. . . . Could you hand me some of those berries? I could smell them in here and I haven't eaten since breakfast."

Phillipa pushed the half-filled bowl to where his eager hand could reach. Greedily he grabbed at the berries, stuffing them into his mouth. The juice ran down his chin in a stream.

"Why are you here?" What crime could rate a living burial?"

"I was so hungry, Maggie. . . . It was just a little

119

carrot . . . I had it under my bed. I didn't think anyone would care that I had taken one. Malcolm found
it. He called me a thief and wouldn't let me have any
luncheon." The little voice was wistful.

"Stand up, gel." The sharp command was punctuated by the prod of a toe in Phillipa's ribs.

Slowly Phillipa rose, her wary gaze meeting Seth's
grin. Never had he seemed so large and solid, and he
was directly between her and safety. It was an indica-
tion of Miss Stanhope-Fredericks's mental state that
her conception of safety was the person of a history
master with dark eyes.

"Well, well, well, if it ain't our fine miss."

"What sort of creature are you, putting a boy in a
place like that?" Phillipa raged, unmindful of her own
precarious situation.

"Ain't he told ye? He's on punishment. The meals
prepared and served by yer loving hand weren't
enough for his young lordship, so he stole. Don't ye
think that's a crime?"

"The crime is in serving meals like that to children
in the first place!" Phillipa spoke impulsively, her
bottled-up feelings finally finding voice. "There is no
reason why such poor fare should be on the table.
The fees here—"

A hard fist grabbed her wrist and she was pulled
uncomfortably close to him, close enough to smell his
fetid breath and the cheap scent he used. "Ah, ye
think ye knows so much. . . . A gel like ye shouldn't
think of anything but pleasing a man. And I bet ye
knows how, too. . . ."

His lips, eager and moist, descended on hers.

Outraged at such an assault, Miss Stanhope-

Fredericks reacted on an instinctual level, kicking and scratching like a wild beast, landing several surprisingly solid body blows and laying open the monitor's cheek with her nails. He drew back in surprise, felt the blood on his face, and the ugly eyes went to slits.

"Wild one, ain't ye? Well, the proper place for wild ones is in a cage!" Dragging Phillipa behind him, Seth stalked to the other side of the punishment box, where a great heavy door lay almost flat on the ground, fastened to an equally massive frame with a huge sliding bolt. The apparatus would seem to have been in fairly continuous use, for it opened easily even with his one hand, the gaping black entrance looking like a grave. "And ye can stay there until ye rot!" Seth roared and flung Phillipa down the shallow steps, then slammed and locked the door with an awesome finality.

"I say, Maggie, are you all right? That was a nasty tumble." Tiny hands aided Phillipa into a sitting position. She tried to catalog her bruises and consciously ignore the hovering dark, broken only by a tiny shaft of light filtering in through the grating.

"I think so. Nothing seems to be broken. What a horrible hole this is."

"Yes," Ian said staunchly, trying to be a brave and protective male, but his years betrayed him and his hand slid into Phillipa's. "It's not so bad now that you're here." Then, "Do you think we will die here?"

"Of course not," Phillipa answered with more courage in her voice than in her heart. "What made you ask that?"

"People have died here before."

With an uncanny certainty Phillipa suddenly knew that here were some of the answers that she had been

121

seeking so diligently, but had he to mention them now, here? It made it seem as if they were not the only ones in the small cellar, that it was populated with the numberless, faceless shades of those who had gone before. It was not too foolish a notion when one was locked in a chamber that could very well double for a tomb.

"Who?" She was compelled to ask, even as she knew, for half hints heard and then forgotten came back. Arnold's letters . . .

"Oh, the maid was the last . . . not the one on the stairs, but the one before you came. The boys say the ghosts scared her to death," Ian added with relish. "But she probably had a fever, like the others."

"Any boys?"

"A few," he said, casual about the presence of death. "Ludowe . . . Stanhope-Fredericks . . . I don't know all their names. . . . They always say there's some other cause, though. Mr. Snodgress doesn't want to get in trouble with the governors."

Unbidden, twin tears began to slither down Phillipa's cheeks, leaving streaky trails in the dirt. The question she had been fearing and avoiding formed and slipped from her lips.

"Arnold Stanhope-Fredericks. Did he die because of this hole?"

"Yes. Did you know him, Maggie?"

Phillipa choked back an anguished sob. Once started, it must be finished. "Yes, I knew him. Why . . . how . . . ?"

"He was so brave. . . . He spoke back to Mr. Snodgress . . . said that he was a gentleman's son and would not be treated like this. He said that he was going to write to his father and see that the school was closed. They locked him up and left him here overnight, then asked him if he was still of the same mind. He said yes, that he was a Stanhope-Fredericks and they couldn't hope to make him cry craven so easily."

Phillipa sighed. Yes, that was Arnold, prideful and staunch.

"So they put him back in here for another night," Ian was saying, "and the next morning he was sick with fever. He died two days later."

Now the picture was complete; she had found out what she wanted to know. November was wet and cold and more often than not snowy; even now in spring the walls were damp with slimy moisture. In November . . . Phillipa could not restrain a small sob, for it was as if the scene were being enacted before her eyes.

Arnold, determined and sturdy in his uniform, facing up to the demons in the form of men who ran this place, acting with the courage of a grown man; Arnold being dragged fighting to this place and thrown in; the night, cold and dreadfully damp; the challenge the next day and his defiant answer; another night—Arnold huddling against the wall, trying to get warm; the cold morning; the raging fever. . . . Had he called for his family in his delirium, unable to understand why they did not come to his aid? The fever; had he had any care at all? Finally welcome oblivion and the everlasting sleep.

As if a barrier had been breached, Phillipa's lips formed her brother's name over and over again and at last the tears she had been unable to shed before welled up and flowed. At last she was free to truly mourn her brother.

Ian, showing a tact rare in a boy so young, asked no questions of the weeping girl, but merely stroked her hair as a gesture of comfort, as if he were the senior and she the child. Finally, exhausted by the surfeit of emotion, both prisoners slept, their arms entwined like brother and sister.

CHAPTER FIFTEEN

It had been dark for some time, for the moon was well up and sending a faint, watery light through the tiny grating. Cramped and stiff from the cold and Ian's dead weight curled up in her arms, Phillipa gently stretched as much as possible without disturbing the boy.

For a moment the night was still, with only the soft soughing of the wind to break the quiet. Then the unnatural sound came again and Phillipa knew what it was that had waked her. Someone was opening the door. There was no time to think of a plan of action, no time to wake Ian, no time to do anything save watch the great portal swing up and pour in a flood of watery moonlight.

"Maggie?"

Phillipa exhaled the breath she didn't even know she had been holding. In the dark, in any place, in any time, on any planet, she would have recognized that voice.

"Geraint?"

She pulled free of Ian's weight and scrambled up the steps to the blessed open air and straight into the security of Geraint's arms. His shoulder was strong and, as she had fantasized, just right to lay her head and troubles on. His hand reached up to caress her hair and, finding the detested mobcap, he removed the offending article. Never very securely fastened, Phillipa's hair came unbound and drifted about her shoulders in a chocolate-colored cloud.

"You don't know how I've longed to do that," Geraint said, his voice strangely unsteady. "It never did become you."

"I promise never to wear one again."

"I'll see that you don't. Are you all right?"

"I am now," Phillipa said truthfully from the haven of his arms.

"Maggie?"

Phillipa felt a start of guilt; she had been so involved with her own relief and happiness that she had totally forgotten her small companion. His voice, sleepy and small, drifted up to her.

"Ian! It's all right. Come up."

Loosing her, Geraint reached down into the darkness and pulled up the boy. Somehow he looked smaller in the moonlight, yawning and knuckling his eyes.

"Are you all right?"

"Yes, Mr. Catton."

"Do you think you can get to your bed without being noticed?"

"Yes, sir. But Seth . . . Won't they expect to find me here in the morning?"

"I'll take care of any problems that arise. Go to bed now, and mind! No noise, and don't be noticed!"

"You can depend on me, sir," he said. "Coming, Maggie?"

"I'll take care of Maggie," Geraint said in a voice that made Phillipa's knees feel extremely unreliable. "Go on."

"Yes, sir." In a moment he was gone, visible briefly as little more than a shadow and then not at all.

"Maggie!" Geraint breathed and gathered her back into his arms. "Are you all right? I'm sorry you had such a stay in that beastly place, but it took me so long to find out what had become of you. Are you hurt?"

"I'm all right," she murmured happily into his shoulder. "Now, Geraint, people . . . boys . . . have died because of that place. What is going on here? What sort of a place is this?" Her voice reflected her horror and disgust.

"We've got to get you away from here," Geraint said, adroitly side-stepping her question, an omission that did not really occur to her until much later. "In the morning you're going to leave here."

Phillipa would have spoken, but he went on, ruthlessly making plans. "No arguments. You'll go someplace safe and wait until I finish here and come for you."

"I can't—"

126

"This is no way for us to start, my dear, with you setting your will up against mine." Gentle fingers touched her lips, which were in turn followed by even gentler lips that sweetly turned demanding and passionate. With a flood of feeling from wells so deep that she did not know she possessed them, Phillipa returned his kisses, her body molded to his, her soul asking nothing more than that this moment go on forever.

"I'll send you to my aunt in Bath," Geraint whispered finally. "She'll look after you until I am able to come for you. Then we'll see about our future."

"Our future?"

"Does the idea displease you?"

"No," Phillipa said with a happy sigh. "It pleases me very much."

"Then be ready to travel at first light. I'll take you to Pelton Lea tomorrow. The mail coach stops at the Red Lion and you can take that to Bath. My aunt will be delighted to have you. . . . My love . . ." Again his eager lips pressed hers, and for Phillipa the night birds' singing was nothing less than the hallelujah of a heavenly choir.

Some time later Geraint pulled back, leaving her to stand alone on unsteady legs. "That's enough of that, my girl, or we shall be out here all night. You must get some sleep because tomorrow is going to be a long day for you and I have a full schedule."

Phillipa made an inarticulate sound of disappointment. The fervor of her emotions had served effectively to rob her of the power of spoken communication, and she felt the loss of his arms around her almost as a physical amputation.

"My God, you can drive a man mad, my precious, but remember that we shall soon have a very long time to be together. I shall follow you to Bath as soon as humanly possible, but now there are more things to be done. Can you get back to your attic without being seen?"

"Yes. And you?"

In the moonlight his smile was devilish. "I have things to do. In the morning, then, my sweet. At first light, in the rose garden?" Geraint asked, picking the rose garden from a rare sentimental gesture, remembering it to be the place of their first meeting. He must be getting old and soft to let such a reason appeal to him, but the understanding glow in the woman's eyes made it worthwhile.

Wisely they did not kiss again, not wanting to risk the chance of forgetting all their purposes in a consuming passion, but briefly touched hands and then melted into the shadows.

Phillipa floated as if she were a part of the moonlight itself, darting from shadow to shadow, her feet quite as light as her heart. He loved her, he loved her, he loved her . . . and oh, how she loved him! She wanted to be with him, to laugh with him, to spend every minute at his side, to have him see her as her true self, prettily dressed and coiffed, to meet her family. . . .

That was an unhappy thought. In the glory of Geraint's arms she had forgotten the very reason that had brought her here in the first place. True, she had discovered the true cause of Arnold's death, but she could not leave here with a clear conscience until this dreadful place gave up the last of its secrets.

Her romantic elation completely dissipated, Phillipa took the tinderbox from the cabinet and with a heavy heart made her way to the headmaster's office, knowing in her heart the trepidation of Pandora.

With trembling fingers she lit the stump of a candle on the desk and went directly to the stationery drawer. Her strength and determination did not dare fail her now. She squared her shoulders like a brave soldier, reached beneath the papers, and pulled forth a heavy canvas-bound ledger. Leaning back in the chair and spreading the book open where the flickering candle would illuminate it the most, Phillipa studied the pages with mingled awe and revulsion, for there in sprawling columns was the whole story.

It was a very clever plan and very nearly foolproof; without this book it would be almost impossible to prove any sort of case against Mr. Snodgress and the rest of his unholy crew. This ledger, compared to the "official" one that was kept for the benefit of governors and occasional parents or guardians, was most revealing, for here were the true accounts of St. Gregory's. It was a masterly scheme.

Snodgress had received the exorbitant tuitions and entered them most properly in the formal ledger. Then he had payed quite handsome sums for good food and coal in large amounts, getting a receipt each time so that the whole transaction could be documented. In case any curious guardians or governors should show an interest in the accounts, Mr. Snodgress would be able to show the official book with its neat record of receipts and expenditures, with an entirely fair profit, to the satisfaction of both sides. In the second book, the record of the true state of things,

129

were the accounts of monies received from Mr. Dinsworthy for the fine foods so carefully purchased and the scanty expenditures for the food actually served. Also, the money brought in from the sale of most of the coal and a great deal of the school linens showed up in the columns.

Phillipa's stomach churned unsteadily as she read down the entries. Deliveries had been made to the school on a regular basis and, just as regularly, supplies had gone from the school to The Boar's Head in Canton-on-Marley, the last having been the night that Florrie died. Her brain spinning busily, Phillipa leaned back in the chair and thought, the dangerously low candle forgotten. It did not take a great intellect to see what had happened; she had worried a great deal about how she had slept through Florrie's death and now it was fairly obvious. The tea, uncharacteristically offered by Mrs. Manning, had not been a reward for a job well done, but a way to keep her out of the way and ignorant. Doubtless it had been well laced with laudanum or some other opiate to make her sleep through the transaction. Florrie had eaten nothing that day, save the few bites Phillipa herself had brought her. Since she was so very ill, the villains thought her too weak to leave her bed or had forgotten her existence completely. On hearing the noise, Florrie had forced herself out of bed to investigate and had been murdered for what she saw . . . and whom.

It took a few moments of mental gymnastics before Phillipa could divine the reason behind the housekeeper's part in this atrocity. After all, the woman appeared to be on intimate speaking terms with the

Lord, and the Word of the Lord was "Thou shalt not steal." Snodgress would have been too clever to offer her money from the scheme, for nothing would have offended her more. No, he must have been subtle, pretending a piety that matched the housekeeper's own, audibly bemoaning the boys' spiritual attitudes with phrases like "Isn't it a pity that the boys don't appreciate the glories of self-abnegation" or "Those lads think more of their stomachs than of the Kingdom of Heaven." Then he would ask for her opinion on how they could turn the boys from this program of self-indulgence to one of piety and self-denial. Phillipa sighed; Mrs. Manning would have fallen into his hands like a ripe plum! Of course, to her the boys would appear selfish, gluttonous, pleasure-seeking little creatures. She would be more than willing to help save them from the error of their ways. Let them meditate on the pleasures of Heaven, rather than the pleasures of the table! It would, of course, be permissible to starve their little bodies so that their immortal souls might prosper, and, since Mrs. Manning was also very practical, Snodgress would have stressed that it would be false economy to let the good food spoil. To waste it would be a sin, so why not sell it to Mr. Dinsworthy at The Boar's Head? The money could be put to so many good uses. . . . Phillipa felt acutely ill.

And Geraint? Just how deeply was Geraint involved in this?

With no warning the door was flung open, the draft knocking out the poor candle stub; it made no matter, however, for the intruders carried their own illumination, which revealed their faces more than plainly.

"Well, well," Snodgress said, in a horrible parody of

131

geniality. "What do we have here? Surely this isn't our little serving wench, prowling through private papers!"

"She's got the book," the head monitor hissed, a thread of fear in his voice.

"Be calm, Seth. There is no need for panic, for we have the situation well in hand. She might have read the book, but that makes no difference."

"How do you know she's the only one? She might have showed it—"

Snodgress scowled. "Think, man! Use the few brains the Creator gave you. She's still here, isn't she? And so's the book. If she'd taken it away, why bring it back? They'd try to protect the evidence."

"Yes, sir," Seth muttered.

"And now for you, missy." Snodgress moved forward until only the desk separated him from Phillipa. She was frozen to her seat, unable to move even if she hadn't been encumbered with the heavy book. "I must admit that this isn't a surprise; your appearance here was never quite as it should be. Give me the ledger."

Phillipa calmly closed the book and placed it in the headmaster's outstretched hands. Above all, she must remember who she was and act accordingly. If it were God's will that she die now, let her die in a way that would be an honor to her name and breeding.

"You won't get away with it, Snodgress," she said evenly.

"And who's going to tell?" he replied with a sneer.

Phillipa took a deep breath and made her last effort. "It's already too late. Sir Percy Hightower knows of your infamous scheme and is even now . . ." she said, unconsciously coming very close to the truth.

"Hightower!" Seth murmured, and even Snodgress paused. "How did she know his name?"

Ruthlessly Phillipa pursued her slim advantage; every moment spent talking was one more moment she remained alive. "I know a great deal, and so does he. The Board of Governors—" She stopped at the sight of the headmaster's smile.

"My grannie used to say that what can't be cured must be endured, and when you've done all you can, you can't do anymore; wise woman, my grannie. I think the days of my tenure at Saint Gregory's are over."

Miss Stanhope-Fredericks had but a moment to mull over his cryptic remarks before the headmaster stepped forward, raised his hand, and plunged her painfully into darkness.

Yes, thought the headmaster, *almost any circumstance could be turned to the use of a clever man.* For some time he had suspicioned that the authorities were a little more interested in the affairs of St. Gregory's than they should have been, and the selection of an escape route had seemed prudent.

From under the clothespress the headmaster brought a small tin box and proceeded to stuff his pockets with the bills it contained. It could have been much less a sum had he not been a clever man, for with true foresight and expectation of either the injudicious spending of the monitors—which might have caused comment—or the need of a hasty flight, he had withheld most of their share in trust for such a time as they were ready to make their way in the world. And they had believed him!

A faint, acrid smell reached his nostrils; apparently Seth was doing his job. Very little of the Comedy of St. Gregory's remained to be acted out. In a few moments he would rouse the boys—nasty, vulgar creatures, boys—and hurriedly save them from the fire. The monitors would have been instructed by now to act in character, checking on the children and staff and trying to save the building, ostensibly being the perfect student assistants. Doubtless the town folk would hear the fire bell and rush to help save the children. In the ensuing confusion Ira Snodgress would disappear and later be reborn in some distant city with a new identity. With luck, they might even think the charred bones of the scullery his.

CHAPTER SIXTEEN

It was the smoke that woke her, thick and black, roiling in foglike fashion, filling her nose, lungs, and eyes; for a moment she could not think where she was. The pulsating red light, the thick atmosphere, the heat, were all alien. As consciousness returned odd fancies filled her mind: If Snodgress had killed her, then was this eternity? How ironic that she had never before really believed in Hell.

Greedily the flames chewed at the dusty draperies,

134

exploding into a blinding column of fire, and Phillipa finally and thoroughly woke up. The place was an inferno; fire adorned the walls and danced madly over the furniture in an orgy of destruction. Beneath her the floor was hot and in a moment of horror Phillipa realized that she had not been supposed to wake up, that this was to have been her fate. Sheer instinct propelled her to her feet; she could not just lie there, waiting for the surety of death . . . she had to get out. . . .

Waves of unbearable heat assailed her in the hallway; here the smoke was worse, a dense, impenetrable curtain ruffled only by the grasping flames. Again Phillipa fought a rising panic and forced herself to think logically. Ahead, the main stairwell was like a chimney, filled by a column of flames. Around her feet the floor was growing hotter and hotter; soon it would be in flames and she . . .

The thought sent her feet into motion almost before her head responded. With the speed of the desperate, Phillipa dashed through the burning maw of the corridor, making herself as small as possible to avoid the greedy tentacles of fire. The service stairs were just ahead; they were small and steep, but they were in the oldest part of the building and made of stone. If the roof were still holding there and if she could get through the kitchen, she might have a chance.

Inside the service stairs it was hot and airless; Phillipa fought to retain her consciousness against the poisonous atmosphere and her footing on the worn, twisting steps. She could feel her skin cracking and blistering in the intense heat.

Her luck seemed to have held. The kitchen was still

135

fairly intact, but the ceiling was an undulating sheet of flame. Seconds later and she would surely have been too late; now she could measure in feet the distance to life and freedom. . . .

She ran, sprinting across the cracked old flags, the door coming closer and closer. . . .

With a roar that was a grotesque parody of fiendish laughter, Phillipa's luck ran out and the ceiling fell, covering her with debris that singed her skin and laid a great smoldering beam across her shoulders, blistering them black. Phillipa screamed, writhing helplessly.

Centuries, aeons later, the weight lifted and strong hands, themselves now marked by fire, pulled her up and out of the building, into the night air, which was only a little less thick with smoke.

"Steady, my precious, we'll get you out of this."

Geraint's voice; how strange that she should acquire a belief in both Hell and miracles in such a short time. A soft sigh escaped her scorched throat and she gently laid her head against his shoulder. Now everything would be all right. Geraint had come for her; she was alive and in his arms. . . .

The stabbing of the cool, night-dewed grass against charred and raw flesh brought her to full and painful awareness once more. Geraint's face above hers looked like a mummer's, blackened and streaked by soot and tears. She tried to speak his name, but no sound would come from between her cracked lips.

"Hush, my darling . . . it's all right. . . . You're going to be all right. . . ." Gently his lips brushed hers, and she would have gladly borne ten times the pain for the love and sweetness contained in that small contact. "I have one more thing to do, then I'll come back for you and we'll find you help. No one will hurt you again. Can you wait for me?"

Phillipa nodded and gave a travesty of a smile. At the prospect of a lifetime with Geraint she could wait forever, no matter the cost. Involuntarily she shivered in the evening chill and Geraint rose, stripping off the singed jacket he wore. It was poor cover, but it would do until he could arrange something more suitable.

A figure moved in the shadows, poorly illuminated in the unsteady light of the burning school, but visible enough to show clearly the blanching of the headmaster's face at the sight of the girl, burned and blackened but alive, lying on the ground. Like a specter risen from the grave to accuse the living guilty, she raised a smudged hand and uttered strange, dry cries. Her companion, barely recognizable as the history master, seemed to divine her unspoken denunciation and, despite his hindering limp, lunged.

Ira Snodgress was an obsessively rational man and, in being so, he laid himself more open to moments of panic. His reaction to the miraculous resurrection of his safely murdered victim was one of supernatural terror. Perhaps if the incident had not happened right in the first glow of pride in a deception well planned, if he had not been so sure of the chit's inevitable demise, if it had not occurred in the theatrical, Gothic light of the burning building, Mr. Snodgress would have been better able to handle it. As it was, his emotions reacted before his logical mind and he ran. Escape was still possible, if he were clever and daring enough. The path past the punishment box . . .

The path was blocked and to his horror the headmaster recognized at least one of the grim group of men. In the flaring light the face of Sir Percy Hightower, head of the Board of Governors, was set and hard. Panicked or not, Snodgress was still rational enough to know that there was only one action left to him. With a sound like laughter, Ira Snodgress wheeled about and ran headlong into the blazing structure just as the rooftree gave way, sending the entire building down in an explosive blast.

The history master too recognized the party on the path and walked toward them, his jaw clenched.

Phillipa, safe behind a screening curtain of shrubs, saw the demise of the school, but was unable to see that the villainous headmaster had himself suffered the fate planned for her. The entire scene had become dreamlike and insubstantial. Floating in and out of a delirious consciousness, Miss Stanhope-Fredericks thought the face bending over her was a hallucination, until a single tear rolled from his eye and splashed onto her face, leaving a damp trail in the soot.

"Father."

"Phillipa, Phillipa . . . you're alive. May the Lord be praised! Come . . . I have a berlin . . . We'll take you home." Mr. Stanhope-Fredericks cast aside the dirty coat that covered her and tenderly wrapped his daughter in the blanket that he had feared would be her shroud. He had been fortunate in that no one had seen him. Now he could take Phillipa home with no one the wiser and, with just a little bit of luck, no one would ever know about her escapade. Once they were clear of the area unobserved, her reputation would be safe.

Her father's haste disturbed Phillipa's precarious grip on consciousness. She tried to tell him that they should wait, that Geraint would expect to find her here, that he must come with them, but she couldn't make him hear her through the encroaching black fog, and at the last she neither felt nor saw nor thought anything.

Sir Percy Hightower recognized the limping form coming toward him and extended his hand only to recoil. "Ludlowe! Your hands—"

"They're not bad, sir. I presume you received my report?"

"Yes, but just a bit too late, it seems. By his actions Snodgress has confirmed them and placed himself before a higher judgment than ours."

"A fitting death," the history master said with venomous emphasis.

"We checked out your reports about the food sold to the innkeeper. It took a time to get the man to talk, but he corroborated it finally," Sir Percy said through clenched teeth. He had waited months to get proof against Snodgress, planted Ludlowe in the school as a master to expedite investigations, and had looked forward with unjudiciary enthusiasm to confronting the headmaster with his crimes, all to be balked at the last moment.

"Did you get the rest?"

"All but one; a lout named Seth . . ."

"One of the monitors," Ludlowe answered Sir Percy's implied question. "Cunning lad."

"That fits with what we've been told. Seems he was a bit smarter than the rest and didn't wait around . . . just took off. We'll post a reward, of course. . . ."

Ludlowe frowned. "I doubt if it will do any good. He wasn't one of the masterminds anyway, just a hireling. Be good if you could catch him, though. All the boys out?"

The older man nodded. "Yes, they're taken care of. Luckily no one was seriously injured, it seems. Tomorrow we'll start returning them to their guardians and parents."

"They're the lucky ones." Involuntarily the history master's eyes misted at the memory of his beloved little brother and of his fate at the hands of Snodgress. For a moment he sincerely regretted that the building itself had had the pleasure of destroying such a creature when he had wanted the distinction so badly himself.

"Well, that's about all we can do tonight. Can we give you a ride back to the village? Best get those hands seen to . . ."

"No, there is more to be done here." With a slight bow Ludlowe took leave of his superior and hurried back to where he had left Maggie. At least she was safe, he thought. No one would be looking for her now. He could take her someplace where she could be treated and they could start their life together free of suspicion . . .

Ludlowe had never been considered a stupid man; therefore it was easy for him to deduce from the chit's absence that since she had been unable to walk by herself and there was no sign of a struggle, she had gone voluntarily with the only missing member of the unholy crew.

Seth.

140

With a barrage of curses Ludlowe picked up his coat, so contemptuously left behind, and walked off into the dark, muttering bitter invective against the perfidy of women.

CHAPTER SEVENTEEN

Later Phillipa could never really remember exactly when she regained full consciousness and memory. There was a vague memory of pain and a jolting carriage ride, ending with someone crying. . . . Then there was her own bed in her own room at Worthington Grange and Mother was there, and Kirky, and Father, and oddly enough, Letty. There was day and night and pain and the doctor from Eaton-on-the-Weir, who gravely shook his head, and then darkness. . . . And somewhere in the recesses of her mind there was a silent cry for a dark-eyed history master.

It was autumn before Phillipa was allowed to leave her room. After much pleading she was finally carried by a sturdy footman to a chaise in the garden, securely wrapped in shawls against any vagrant chill and allowed to sit in the afternoon sun, surrounded by roses drooping in the season's final show. The conversation flowed around her in pleasant eddies; it was a happy family group. Mr. and Mrs. Stanhope-

Fredericks were gratified that their elder child had been spared and returned to them. Kirky was delighted to be returned to the home that was so much more her own than her sibling's had been. And Letty, for the first time a member in a happy, affectionate family, was blossoming with love and warmth as if she had belonged there always.

"Did you remember to speak to the housekeeper about the guest room, Kirky?" Mrs. Stanhope-Fredericks asked.

"Yes, ma'am. All is in readiness."

"Are we to have company?"

"Oh, my dear, you were asleep when the message came. Your aunt Beatrice and Ronnie are coming for a visit."

"Ronnie, Mother? Is he back from Spain?"

Her mother nodded. "Yes, he's on leave . . . has been trying to locate a friend of his, I believe. Anyway, he was most desirous of seeing you, but he waited until you were strong enough to receive him."

Phillipa smiled for the first time in weeks. "Oh, it will be good to see Ronnie again! He's been gone ever so long. Did you ever meet him, Letty?"

Lady Lettice looked up from a particularly complicated piece of embroidery. "No, I haven't had the honor. I've heard you speak of him, of course, but unless I'm mistaken he went to the Peninsula before we came out."

"Oh, of course. I had forgotten. You'll like him. For most of our childhood his family lived over at Lakelands, just a few miles from here. We used to have such fun together."

Mrs. Stanhope-Fredericks, her reminiscences of

childhood escapades not as pleasant as her daughter's, frowned. "You two got into more trouble than any six children should have."

Phillipa laughed, a sound that was heavenly to her loved ones' ears. Already Ronnie was good for her. "Remember the time we played knight, Kirky?"

The old nurse snorted. "Indeed I do! Playing in that old tower, and me having to rouse half the county!"

Letty's eyes opened wide. "What happened?"

"Ronnie and I were playing knight—well, he was the knight and I was his squire. We couldn't have been over ten or so. . . . Anyway, not far from the lake there is a tumbledown old fortress tower, Norman they say, and as good knights we had to defend it. Part of the old first floor was still there, so we climbed up to see the enemy better and . . . the ladder fell. We had to stay up there until someone came to rescue us."

"And me not knowing where those two were . . . and then about dark their ponies came in without them. I tell you, Miss Phillipa, if every hair on my head isn't gray, it's no thanks to you!"

The implication was an old one and Phillipa smiled indulgently. "When are Aunt Beatrice and Ronnie coming, Mother?"

"Tomorrow, they said. You must take care, dear. I don't want you too tired to see them, nor must they exhaust you. You're still delicate."

Again Mrs. Stanhope-Fredericks had underestimated her daughter. With the high courage and impetuousness that was characteristic of her, Phillipa was standing on her own at the foot of the stairs when

143

the arrival of her aunt and cousin was announced. Not unexpectedly, her appearance caused anxious protestations from her parents—Kirky and Lady Lettice having most properly absented themselves from such an intimate family reunion—but Miss Stanhope-Fredericks merely declared that she was no longer an invalid and refused to appear so missish in front of her old playfellow.

As if he had heard his name mentioned, Lord Ronald Mickleham entered the hall and, with a lack of civility to his elder relatives that would have been shocking under other circumstances, he flew immediately to Phillipa's side, catching her in an affectionate bear hug that threatened her breath. Ronnie was fond of Pia and, though he had been given a sketchy account of her adventures, he was unprepared for the change in her. He supposed that he should be grateful she was at least alive, and told her so when the formalities were finally done and they were alone in the small salon.

Ronnie again held her close and for a moment the pair stood in a long embrace, the embrace of two dearly loving people separated too long and fearing for each other. It was Phillipa who broke away, stumbling to the sofa, wiping at her eyes.

"Enough, Ronnie! One more moment and I shall be soaking your pretty coat."

He dropped to her side with an easy familiarity. "You can ruin any coat I own, Pia."

Impulsively Phillipa grasped her cousin's hand, almost as a lifeline. "Oh, it is so good to see you again. Tell me what you've been doing. Are you a hero?"

"Hardly. I've been called a fool more often than a

hero. Still, I've seen my share of action on the Peninsula. Fact is, I've been hunting for my old cohort Ludlowe while I was in London. Things got devilish flat after he was invalided home."

"He was injured?"

"Yes, badly too. I wrote you about him . . . Paul Ludlowe. I've scoured Town high and low—"

"I can believe the low. Gaming halls and cockpits . . ."

Ronnie scowled and went on. ". . . high and low for him, but no news. His father has a place in Sussex, I believe. If I don't find him on my next trip to London, I shall write for news."

"I do hope nothing untoward has befallen him," Phillipa said conventionally.

"And you, Pia," Ronnie said, leaning forward. "What about you? What has befallen you?" Inwardly he was still trying to assimilate this grave-eyed creature, this fragile invalid, with his memories of a cousin who would take the highest fence, the highest tree, the wildest dare that two children could concoct. Phillipa was silent for a time, so long that her cousin thought her mind had wandered. She was different somehow. It was not just the physical ravages of illness, but something essential in her had changed.

"Pia?"

"I can't believe you don't know, Ronnie."

He nodded uncomfortably and began to toy with one of the gilt buttons adorning the front of his jacket. "I know some, I'll admit that, but I'd like to hear the whole story. From you. Why did you do such a harebrained thing, Pia? Didn't you realize what you'd be risking?"

"I thought that of all people you'd understand, Ronnie!" Phillipa's reply was almost a cry. "Don't you see? I did it for Arnold. How could I worry about parties and whether or not I would be received at Almack's when little Arnold's murderers were going unpunished? Father never intended us to know what happened there. If I hadn't heard him foxed and raving about murderers and villains that horrible night, I'd never have known. But I did know, Ronnie, and I had to do something about it."

"Didn't he tell you that Hightower and the Board of Governors had some operative in there?"

Pia shook her head. "No, he never mentioned it to me. I don't know what became of the letter. Maybe he burned it or something. He never knew he let anything slip until later, when he came for me, and we've never mentioned it since then, save when he assured me that all the villains were caught or dead . . . in the fire." Her words came with an effort, remembering the afternoon when Mr. Stanhope-Fredericks, hoping to ease his daughter's mind, had promised her that all were accounted for. It was just a small fabrication, designed to make her rest easy, for Mr. Stanhope-Fredericks never thought the one escaped villain would dare to cross paths with them again. As a doting father, he took her tears to be those of relief.

"Don't you see, Ronnie, I couldn't do anything else," Phillipa finished, her eyes searching his face, their troubled depths clouded with tears. She had never dreamed that Ronnie would join the censure against her. If he didn't understand, the world was riven, there was no camaraderie or justice . . .

Softly she began to recount the events of her adventures, already misty and dreamlike in her mind, stating only the facts, trying not to let the mention of Geraint affect her voice. When she came to the tale of the punishment box, Ronnie's fingers tightened convulsively, his knuckles white, and when her voice finally broke describing the fire, his arms went around her and held her fast.

"Pia! Darling, brave, idiotic. . . . You could have been killed!"

"I almost was. The boys got away . . . I was caught by a burning beam. The history master saved my life." She could say no more; again her ears rang with the scream of the fire and the softness of Geraint's voice.

"I wish I could thank him."

Phillipa straightened and dabbed her eyes, fighting for control. "I do wonder what Mother and Aunt Beatrice are about, chatting so long. Do you think they've forgotten us?"

"Dear innocent," Ronnie said in the old railing tone of childhood. "They will leave us alone as long as possible."

"You can't mean . . ."

"Oh, I do, cousin. I was given a highly expurgated version of your little prank—yes, they called it just that, a prank—and a lecture by my mother. 'Phillipa is a good girl, though she is given somewhat to high spirits. However, I feel sure that once married she will settle down admirably' . . ." Ronnie's mimicry of his mother's tone was both uncanny and unkind.

"They want us to make a match of it?"

"They wouldn't be averse. I can see their point. Our estates match together, there would be a considerable melding of fortunes. I realize that marriage between first cousins isn't quite the thing, but under the circumstances they're prepared to overlook that."

Pia swallowed heavily. Were things as bad as that? "Ronnie, I love you dearly, but marriage?"

"Yes, it does seem a bit incestuous, since we grew up almost as brother and sister, doesn't it? Still, I can't think they're all too serious about it . . . just an idea. It will pass."

Phillipa began to weep in earnest. "They want to get rid of me . . . to get me settled in a hurry, as if I were damaged goods! I'm not, Ronnie, I'm not!"

Lord Ronald pulled his cousin close and wiped away the tears. "I know you aren't, darling. You're the purest, loveliest thing I've ever seen. And I'm saying that because I love you, not because I'm in love with you. Quite frankly I pity the man you do marry. You'll lead him a pretty dance!"

"I shall never marry," Phillipa wailed with an awful certainty.

"Pia! What do you mean by that? Are you in love with someone? Has he hurt you? Just tell me and I'll call him out if he won't marry you."

The fierce expression on her cousin's face brought a thin edge of laughter and Phillipa leaned back. "No, it can't be like that, dear Ronnie. Your chivalry is for naught."

"You look pale. Do you feel all right?" Ronnie passed his hand over her damp forehead. "Are you feverish?"

"I'm fine. Just a little warm . . ."

"Well, no wonder, the way you're bundled up. All that material up around your neck. . . . It can't be healthy."

"I have to wear high collars, Ronnie, at least for now. Otherwise the scars would show and cause comment," Phillipa said evenly, and saw her cousin go pale. She rushed on. "The beam, you see . . . it fell across my back and shoulders. It's not very pretty."

It took a moment, but the tension drained from him and he looked deeply into his cousin's face. Now it was a woman who faced him, a passionate, mature woman who in so many ways resembled his harum-scarum little cousin and yet . . . "Tell me, Pia . . . this man you love. Does he love you?"

Her moist eyes fixed on the past—Geraint carrying her from the fire, Geraint's lips, Geraint's words . . . but none for her, not really. He had pledged his love to a mysterious creature with no past, someone mendaciously called Maggie, and because of this, Miss Phillipa Stanhope-Fredericks had no future.

"No, not really."

"Then he is blind and—I say, Pia, the history master?"

Phillipa flushed. "Am I so transparent, then?"

"You never could keep a secret from me."

"Oh, Ronnie, it is so good to have you here. I've been alone for so long."

Gently he kissed her forehead. "We're always together, Pia. I'll always be there when you need me. And, I promise you this, dearest coz. I'll find that history master for you, if that's what you want, and be damned to those old cats at Almack's."

For one moment Miss Stanhope-Fredericks's face

shone with the blazing light usually seen in those offered a glimpse of Heaven, then it faded to a frown.
"But he didn't love me, Ronnie, not Phillipa. It is all
right for a history master to love a serving wench, but
when he finds out the truth. . . . And it really
doesn't matter, for Father says that everyone with the
school is now in jail or dead."

"If he actually thought you were nothing more than
a kitchen maid, he hasn't got eyes to see nor brains to
think with! Don't underestimate him, Pia, not if he
was as clever as you say. I'll find him for you, I promise that!" Ronnie said bracingly. Then, to make it as
binding as possible between the two cousins, he
added, "Knight's honor."

Pia smiled at the old code word from their play
days. "I'm glad you're here, Ronnie," she said with
a trusting simplicity that sent her cousin's brain reeling
into plots of prisoners smuggled out of castles and
across the oceans to build new lives. . . . It was a
heady, heroic line of thought that was shattered by
the soft opening of the salon door to admit an angel.

"Oh, I'm sorry, Phillipa, I knew you were with your
cousin, but somehow I thought you were in the drawing room. I just came down to retrieve my book . . .
please excuse . . ." Words tumbled in charming profusion from Letty's mouth. Of course, she had been
privy to the general family gossip of the hoped-for betrothal between Phillipa and her cousin, but she
hadn't expected the cousin to be such a tall, incredibly handsome man, and now, standing there with the
light just so . . .

Phillipa had, of course, read of the phenomenon of
love at first sight, but she had always had the good

sense to think it merely a literary affectation. She had never expected it to be enacted in the small salon of Worthington Grange late on an autumn afternoon. Somewhere within her a small bubble of amusement rose to life again. "Come in, Letty. This is my cousin Ronnie. He has come to squire us both through the London Season," she said most properly. But neither of them seemed to notice her.

CHAPTER EIGHTEEN

With a tug at his cravat Paul Ludlowe stepped from the carriage and looked at the house; there was still time to leave, but he didn't even consider it. Ronnie had been right when he had insisted on Ludlowe's attendance.

Their reunion had been a happy one. During an infrequent visit to White's, Ludlowe had learned of his friend's return to England and both had talked at loud length about their recent doings. At least, Ludlowe reflected, Ronnie had talked. He himself had too much to hide, too many scars to parade his feelings openly. Instead he talked vaguely of his rustic doings at Greathill and of his retired life in Town.

"After all, old man, you aren't the only one with a Peninsular wound; they're quite stylish this year. You can't bury yourself forever, hiding out like a damned hermit!" Ronnie had stormed on hearing of Ludlowe's third refusal to an entertainment, including a definite request from a certain barque of frailty to a private party at Vauxhall Gardens. "And as for the other . . . well, life's for the living, and your little brother would be the first one to say so, I'm sure, though I never met him, but he still would if he were any kind of a brother at all."

"You're right, he would," Ludlowe had said finally, feeling the knife twist in the core of his being, the double-edged blade of the loss of his brother and the ineradicable feelings that still fermented over the two-faced doxy who had called herself Maggie and who had profited from the agony of small boys. But Ronnie was right, as he had an infuriating habit of being, and there was the question of the succession. It was his duty to provide an heir to Greathill, especially now since Laurence was gone, and there were no other relatives except for an obscure branch of cousins in Devonshire, who had married into trade. He loved the old house and the wandering farms too well to see them come under the stewardship of some hardfisted merchant's brood. To fulfill the succession, however, he would perforce have to find a wife. No matter how unconventional he might be, though, there would be no way he could set up an adventuress and scoundrel as the future Viscountess of Amesfield, no matter how he longed for her and despised himself for doing so. The wench had entangled herself so in his heart that it would be unfair to whatever poor damsel he chose, but Ludlowe could not trust himself to think of that . . . only the succession could be considered. Hopefully he could find some sensible female of impeccable breeding and social acceptability who would not have any romantical notions of love and passion and with whom he could contrive to live a comfortable life. No doubt there would be any number of young ladies capable of finding the future title of viscountess much more attractive than declarations of undying affection and sirupy poetic effusions of love.

"Good evening, sir."

"Evening, Crawford. Looks like a squeeze."

Lady Masham's butler, properly gratified by the fact that his humble name had been remembered by so illustrious a guest, bowed a little more deeply than usual. "I am proud to say that her ladyship's gathering is quite well attended, my lord."

Divested of his hat and wrap, Ludlowe stood aside, observing the milling crowd with wary hesitation, as a wise swimmer will inspect alien water before entering. It was a glittering turnout. In one room alone he could see a good half of the ton—the highest half, of course—and the light refracting from the assembled jewels was blinding. With grace he pressed through the throng, trying to protect his still troublesome wound as unobtrusively as possible, nodding civilly to all and greeting the few old friends he saw . . . so many gone now! Salamanca, Bajados, Ciudad Rodrigo, the blood baths of the Peninsular War, all brought on by the insane ambitions of one Corsican corporal. To make matters worse, now there was the conflict flaring up with the United States, taking away land and sea forces badly needed to keep Wellington from being driven back into the sea. . . .

"Paul! Come here!"

With the uncomfortable knowledge that he had been woolgathering, Ludlowe snapped back immediately into the present. No one could mistake that voice. For months it had driven him mad, soft and purring in his ear, following him with sweet insistence, oddly attracting and repelling at the same time. He could see her now, floating toward him from the ballroom in a direct course as if they had been the only two people in the house, as usual a vision, dressed tonight in varied shades of peach and silver and bedecked in an opulent display of diamonds. Obediently he went to her side and bowed over the small white hand extended to him, barely visible under an encrusting of jewels.

"Your servant, Your Grace."

"Oh, stuff! There's no need to say that. You have never been my servant and have never paid the slightest attention to my wishes." Then, in a different, more intense tone, "I heard you were back. Why haven't you come to see me?"

Ludlowe sighed. At least one thing hadn't changed in his absence. "My time in Town has been short, Your Grace. I have had no occasion to make morning calls and renew old acquaintanceships."

"That is not what I meant, Paul, and you know it. From the first moment I knew you were back I waited for you." She looked up at him with pale-blue eyes, artistically touched with only a hint of tears. She was still as lovely as he had remembered, and it was hard to believe that a dainty faerie creature like her could have a grown daughter and such a reputation.

Again her small hand, frail and white, clung in a calculatedly appealing gesture to his sleeve. Gently he

154

removed it, planted a cool, remote kiss on the fingers, and let it fall.

"I thought we settled that long ago, my dear. Now may I escort you back to your party? Or would you prefer the dowagers' dais? I hear your daughter is in her . . . what is it . . . ? her third Season?"

For a moment she stiffened, her knuckles going white around the sticks of the delicate lace fan, then, deliberately, she relaxed, and said with a demeanor that could chill a room, "No, that will not be necessary. I doubt we will have occasion to meet again."

Paul watched her graceful retreat with a sense of relief. He did not know if it would be any more uncomfortable to have her as an enemy than as a pursuer, but whatever the cost, it was worth it, for his innate fastidiousness of soul would never have permitted him to become a member of the procession passing through the Duchess of Connaught's bed.

The country dance was in the middle of its most intricate and exhausting figure, the dancers weaving and turning energetically to the music. Ludlowe had taken part in similar romps himself, swinging the ladies with pleasure, never once committing the solecism of forgetting the figure, and on occasion showing an ungenteel display of energy. Of course, any participation now was precluded by his wound, but Ludlowe was surprised how much pleasure he got merely by watching the dance and following the half-remembered steps in his mind. It did not seem so long ago that he had danced in this brilliantly lit ballroom and so many others like it. Even the dancers seemed familiar—perhaps not so much in individual personality as in type—almost like an opera with its stock characters. There was the dashing Hussar, the pudgy and perspiring debutante in white, the desperate girl in her third or fourth Season, trying too hard not to end up as an ape-leader, the . . .

Ludlowe pressed hard against the pillar that supported him, alert and wary eyes searching among the entanglement of dancers for another glimpse of the tall brown-haired girl in the yellow dress. *Surely*, he thought, *surely it is nothing more than a trick of the mind, triggered by some chance resemblance! When she comes into sight again I shall laugh at ever having thought her to resemble Maggie at all. It is only that my mind is so full of her that* . . .

The country dance made the final pattern and ended. Politely the participants clapped and began moving away in couples, mingling with the couples from the other dissolving figures, but despite the crowd Ludlowe had no difficulty in singling out his quarry.

Of a certainty it had to be the same girl. She was clean now, well-dressed and coiffed, but surely there would not be two with such grace and height, such purity of feature, so similar as to be identical twins. The proud tilt of the patrician head daring the world to challenge her, so incongruous in a scullery wench, seemed most natural here, as was the grace with which she wore the yellow gown. The gown, while obviously expensive and fabricated by a master hand, was oddly disquieting, some small part of Ludlowe's professional mind noted, for although both beautiful and stylish, it was subtly different from any other gown in the room. A small detail, but then Ludlowe had been justly famed for his attention to small details. It was the neckline, he decided, that set the gown apart. It was high and almost childish, giving a decided air of virginal innocence. *All the better to trap her next victim,* he thought savagely, then as he turned full attention to her escort, his heart suddenly began to thud with painful regularity. Of course he recognized the figure, for hadn't that face become as familiar as his own during the time they had shared the danger and excitement of Peninsular service? Of all the men in the country, the chit would expend her wiles over Lord Ronald Mickleham.

Her pale face smiled up into his tanned one and with casual familiarity Ronnie took her arm and with a pat linked it through his own. They made an extraordinarily handsome couple. As Ludlowe watched their progress across the room from narrowed eyes, they seemed to greet and be greeted by almost everyone.

Ludlowe sighed; he had underestimated the chit, obviously a dangerous mistake to make. In a comparatively short time she had apparently conquered the nigh insuperable bastions of Society and seemed to be fairly well entrenched. Suddenly he remembered the last days at St. Gregory's and felt that he could no longer breathe the same air she did. Still careful not to draw undue attention to himself, he reclaimed his wraps from an impassively surprised Crawford and, declining his carriage, stepped out into the night.

Lord Paul Ludlowe, also at times known as Pablo, would have had his faith in his powers of concealment and discretion severely tested had he been able to read the thoughts of the Duchess of Connaught at that particular moment.

Eustacia's lips tightened to an ugly line, momentarily making her look every minute of her age. That girl again, that same girl who had befriended Letty, making her talk back to her mother, had messed up the match she had personally arranged between Letty and Lowood. Now Paul left immediately after seeing her, for all the world like a frustrated lover. The idea that that girl could have such an effect on the man Eustacia so desired, and the man who had so far resisted her charms, was galling. Twice the Stanhope-Fredericks chit had interfered with Eustacia and no one offended the Duchess of Connaught twice without reprisal. No one!

Made blind by the tumult of his feelings, Ludlowe saw none of the turmoil his going raised in the duchess's breast, but instead he merely struck out into the dark. He had been a fool not to see the girl's design earlier. Of course she would head for London. With her air of breeding, it would not be difficult to masquerade as a lady of quality, and naturally a wealthy and titled husband would be her next object. Had he not been so closely involved in the tangle, he would have greatly enjoyed the spectacle of Fashionable London taking a scullery wench into the fold. The question was, how could she have accomplished it so quickly? Money opened doors, but could she have gotten that much as her share?

No . . . but she and Seth could have. With their resources pooled they could have put on a little town bronze, found some impoverished beldam on the fringe of Society who would be willing to sponsor the chit and not be too inquisitive into her supposed lineage. Then, once ensconced in Society, they only had to wait until a wealthy, susceptible male came along. With Maggie's looks that wouldn't take long, Ludlowe thought bitterly, remembering with pain the way her eyes could twist a man's being.

Well, she had to be stopped and that was that. And in a way that would not wound Ronnie. There was no use anyone else coming out injured from this hellish mess. If he could save Ronnie from that female's toils heart-whole, he could concentrate on seeing that she and Seth received the full weight of justice. But how?

Ludlowe slowed his step in deference to the fierce ache in his leg. Foolhardy to have come so far! The worsening weather had turned into a steady rain. He looked around and instantly realized just how far he must have walked in his blind fury, for Boodle's was just around the corner. Although a member, he cared little for gaming and seldom attended, but at least he could thaw out, get a drink, and send for a carriage to take him home. Years of service in the warmer climes of the Peninsula had apparently thinned his blood and left him ill-prepared for the rigors of an English winter.

Later, seated in front of a good fire in an almost deserted parlor, a steaming bowl of punch at his side, Ludlowe's mind returned to the problem of Maggie and young Mickleham. What was it that Ronnie had said that day they met? He had been so enraptured in the throes of new love and predictably silly about it that Ludlowe had only listened to about a third of the effusion of words his young friend had put forth. There had been something about his mother being somewhat disappointed in his choice—but that was nothing to wonder at, for Ludlowe knew that Beatrice, Lady Mickleham, would feel nothing less than a Princess Royal a worthy match for her son. What had he said later? Something about her family . . . yes, that was it. There was some impediment coming from her side of the family, that they disapproved of the match. Clever stroke that, knowing that nothing would whet a lover's ardor more than a hint of unfair opposition.

Well, Ludlowe thought savagely, whatever Maggie and Seth were up to, he would scotch their game!

CHAPTER NINETEEN

As luck would have it, Ludlowe got his chance earlier than he would have dared dream, for the next morning, full of megrims and unworkable plans, he arose earlier than usual and, oddly attracted by the chilly morning, called for his horse and set out for the Park.

Phillipa, risen from a sleepless bed, took one look at the cool, gray morning and longed for the open country around the Grange with an intensity that was almost physical. Dressing quickly, she slipped from the house and ruthlessly bullied the sleepy stableboy into saddling her horse, threatening him with his life if he told anyone where she had gone. It was not quite dawn and no one of importance would be abroad at this hour. Surely she could have a bit of a ride in the Park with no damage to her reputation, unhindered by fashion or an accompanying groom.

In the crisp foggy air the Park had a sense of unreality about it, like a landscape in a dream. Even the trees and walks that she knew so well seemed different and mysterious, like some unexplored world half of fact and half of fancy. At the end of the short path Phillipa turned her mount down the long Row, but held down to a slow trot, as the Row was slick and unsafe underfoot from the night's moisture.

A slight breeze began to disperse the gray mist. From behind her Phillipa heard the sound of quick hoofbeats. Apparently she was not the only early riser and in a flash Phillipa saw her foolishness in coming out alone—she had done it again, impulsive, thoughtless, acting without thinking—and would have given anything to see the stolid figure of Jemson riding behind her.

The other rider was still a little way behind. If she could make the turning by the rhododendron bush, there was a second path, but she would have to hurry, for the fog was clearing fast now under the first rays of sunlight.

Phillipa set the spurs to her horse and was terrified to hear the hoofbeats behind her speed up to a pace that her mount was unable to best. Now there was no doubt that the mysterious rider was after her. Although Phillipa strove to think of a way to escape, she was unable to find a viable plan before the big chestnut animal pulled abreast and a lean, fire-scarred hand reached out and brought the little mare to a halt.

Trembling with a mixture of emotions, Phillipa looked up into the face that had haunted her every hour for months. It was thinner now, the cheekbones more prominent and the jaw tighter, as if it were most often clenched. Then Phillipa's gaze went to his eyes and something within her rolled up and withered, for they were arctic, boring into her with a barely suppressed fury.

"Where were you going in such a hurry? Early for an assignation, isn't it? Or are you just on your way home?"

Miss Stanhope-Fredericks barely restrained herself from lashing his face with her crop. To think that she had wasted so much time mooning over this fellow! she thought angrily, even as her heart writhed.

"Is this the way you always accost a lady?"

His smile was twisted. "I don't make a habit of accosting *ladies*."

"You dare!" Phillipa lashed out with her crop, only to have it wrenched urgently from her grasp. "Release my horse this moment."

"No, my fine young miss. I have a few things to say to you and you will oblige me by hearing them."

Phillipa drew a deep breath and replied in her most quelling manner, "I can think of nothing that you could say to interest me."

"Nothing, indeed. Truly I am a fool, for I should have thought that the first place you would come would be London, with its gaiety and the undeniable attraction of wealthy, foolish young men."

"What concern of yours is it where I go?"

He gave a deep, barking laugh that was wholly without mirth. "Doubtless it will please your female

162

vanity to know that when you disappeared on the night of the fire, I was concerned, thinking that you might be badly hurt, out of your head. . . . It was I who was out of my head, but at least my folly has been brought home with a vengeance! You had me so firmly in your wily little clutches that it was some time before I finally accepted that your disappearance and Seth's escape were timed a little too neatly to be a coincidence."

"Seth?" Phillipa asked, unable to keep the wisp of fear from her voice, which he instantly misinterpreted as guilt.

"Yes, Seth. I haven't seen him yet, but then he isn't as skilled in the drawing room graces as you. Doubtless he is in a proper calling, masquerading as your driver or groom . . ."

The enormity of his accusations rolled in on Phillipa in a black wave. "Seth? And—and I? You think that we worked together? That is the filthiest, most horrible—"

"Don't overact your hand. It isn't ladylike. I don't give a groat if you are working with Seth or alone, but I'm warning you—"

"Warning me!"

He went on relentlessly, recklessly, ignoring the edge in her voice, the emotions of the past months too tightly bottled for too long to hold back any longer. "Last night I saw you with a friend of mine. God help me, I might be too late to save myself from your toils, but I will not let you get your hooks into him!"

"And just who is it that you are so anxious to save from me?"

"Lord Ronald Mickleham."

163

"Ronnie!" Phillipa exclaimed in genuine surprise.

"Yes, and for God's sake don't put on that arch-innocent expression. Half of London saw you dancing and walking hand in hand last night. He's a decent boy and I will see you in Hell before you ruin his life."

"I have no intention of ruining Ronnie's life, or anyone else's."

"Might as well say that you have the intention to quit breathing. Or have you really planned to turn respectable with your share?"

For one full moment Phillipa was unable to take in his unspoken accusation, then when the enormity of it finally sank in, she was engulfed with a flood of emotion stronger than she had ever known. She planted a firm, unexpected kick in the tender part of the big chestnut's side; the reaction was all that she could have wanted. Startled, the big horse reared, perforce making Geraint loose his hold on the mare's bridle in order to control his own mount. In that small, unguarded instant Phillipa ignored her own precarious balance and spurred the little brown mare to such a gallop as the poor beast had never before attempted. Without doubt the chestnut could have overtaken them, but when Phillipa ventured a cautious look behind her, the Park was deserted.

Luck favored Phillipa, for she reached her own room unobserved by family or servants. Tossing the discarded habit into a corner, she wrapped herself in a dressing gown before sprawling most unladylike across the bed, her thoughts in a turmoil.

Geraint Catton in London. And a friend of Ronnie's! Being in a black humor, Phillipa of course put

the worst construction on that. In an effort to entertain her, Ronnie had told her a little of life in the Peninsula, of the thieves and robbers who had been his
daily companions, soldiers who fought not for the
sanctity of England nor the glory of heroism, but for
the plunder and freedom from restraint that war pro-
vided. In fact, just about the only decent person Ronnie had ever mentioned was his great friend Lord
Ludlowe, who seemed to represent every virtue. Had
Ronnie been a little younger and more impression-
able, she would have accused him of blatant hero wor-
ship. No, the fact that Geraint claimed friendship with
Ronnie could only act as a minus in her eyes.

How dare he think she was involved in that horror
at St. Gregory's, accusing her as if she were a common
felon! To hide his own complicity in the affair he
would probably take delight in destroying her, and
even if he did care about the truth, it would be too
late, for she would be irreversibly ruined in the eyes
of Society. Could she go to him, tell him the truth,
and promise to keep his part quiet in exchange for his
silence? No! Not only would he probably not even listen to her, but she could never hide anyone who took
part in an evil like that, no matter at what cost to her.
Her soul could not permit such a blatant act of dis-
honor.

Ronnie? He would be more than happy to do anything in his power to make her happy, as he had once
said, but how humiliating it would be to have to admit to him that the gentle schoolmaster whom she had
adored had metamorphosed into a . . . whatever he
was. The hateful man! How could he think she was
such a low creature as to profit off the misery of

children? How could he think that she would have anything to do with a one such as Seth? How could she have been duped, fooled, blinded so thoroughly?

That was another thing. It was far from comforting to know that Seth had escaped the law. Had she known that, she would never have ventured on a solitary ride. Odds would be that he was far from London, but it was disquieting to know that he was at liberty, no matter where he was.

The day dragged on. The ladies of the house were committed to luncheon with Lady Chessingham. Despite the strain of the morning, Phillipa comported herself well, but Letty saw the tension under the surface and watched her covertly with anxious eyes. It was a small party, for Lady Chessingham lived in a tiny jewel box of a house whose dining room could not encompass more than half a dozen guests. To Phillipa's misfortune, Mrs. Valelyn was among the invited.

How smug the odious creature seemed and how far she had traveled in Society! It was a well-known fact that one of the few failings possessed by dear Lady Chessingham was an addictive predeliction for gossip. Now she was well supplied with innumerable on-dits, thanks to the kindness of the charming Duchess of Connaught, who had introduced her to a distinguished purveyor of that particular commodity, namely her bosom bow, Mrs. Valelyn.

Lady Mickleham and her two charges exchanged almost imperceptible glances on seeing this addition to the party, before going in with their heads high in an impressive phalanx. They made a prettier picture than they knew. Beatrice, though no longer a girl, was still a handsome female and looked quite regal in a morning dress of dark violet decoratively stitched in black. She was currently in one of her periodic fits of half-mourning for her late husband, which she affected when in need of his presence and advice. Heaven only knew what he would have said about this tangle of Phillipa's.

The two girls had chosen less formal walking dresses in anticipation of a stroll in the Park later—Phillipa's in her favorite green with a lime-colored underskirt, and Letty's in a flattering jonquil trimmed with cream. All three ladies wore their clothing with an élan that made many of the other guests sigh inwardly and resolve to bully their mantua-makers just a bit more toward the production of such elegance.

"Lady Lettice, my dear . . . how well you look. Doubtless your mamma picked out that simply ravishing gown? She has such exquisite taste," purred the Valelyn creature, for all the world like a cat with a fresh mouse to torment. However, as she could have had no way of knowing, mice sometimes have surprising courage.

"I am so pleased that you find favor with my poor outfit. In truth, dear Lady Mickleham is responsible for it, as it was she who decided to shop that day. You see, we had called at Mamma's house, but she was . . . out," Letty answered sweetly, hesitating for the most necessary fraction of a second between "was" and "out." Inwardly Phillipa applauded, then smiling, entered the fray.

"I vow the lovely duchess must be in a veritable social whirl recently—which is understandable because she is so beautiful and so lively—for although it is hard to credit, she has been out every time Lady Lettice has tried to call in the past few weeks."

"Mamma always did like to be active," Lady Lettice said charitably with just the correct soupçon of pathos.

"And how does she feel about your staying with dear Lady Mickleham?" asked Lady Chessingham, her eyes unabashedly glittering. Never had she expected such action so soon! She could dine out for weeks simply on the strength of being present when the clash between the Mickleham faction and the Connaught faction came. Something pretty smoky—to use a lamentable cant term picked up from her nephew—was going on; the Winterthorpe chit staying with Lady Mickleham while her own mother was living at the family house not two squares away, the girl still publicly and unabashedly single after all the puffery her mother had put up about her marrying the Duke of Lowood. And what was that business about the Stanhope-Fredericks girl being ill or in an accident or something like that? Hadn't dear Mrs. Valelyn said that there was something about that which wasn't quite as it should have been?

Beatrice recognized Lady Chessingham's tactics, having used the same ones on occasion when necessary, and replied, "The duchess has been most gracious about sharing her daughter with me. The duke and I were in long correspondence about it and after careful discussion decided that since the girls are so attached to each other, it seemed simple to have them both stay with us. Lady Lettice was a true godsend in keeping Phillipa's spirits up during her convalescence. I'm afraid the tragedy in the family is still painful to all of us. For the longest time the doctors, and we, feared that my sister would never get over it."

"I hear that you were ill later, my dear. Afterward," Mrs. Valelyn said smoothly to Phillipa. "In the spring." Her tone was a challenge.

Miss Stanhope-Fredericks looked up and smiled. "Yes, I was. Letty was so very kind as to come and bear me company. She kept me from being such a charge on my family, as I am somewhat fretful, I fear."

"So devoted," the Valelyn murmured.

"Both girls are a delight. I always regretted not having any daughters, and now I have two, both such lovely girls," Lady Mickleham said, daring any opposition. Then, with practiced social ease she moved the conversation into safer tracks, namely the Princess Charlotte's coming of age next year and speculations on the so far unforthcoming marriage which, as Heiress Apparent, she would be expected to make.

CHAPTER TWENTY

"Mrs. Valelyn is an odious, prying wretch!" Phillipa fumed, setting a pace that was both unladylike and difficult for the smaller Letty to maintain.

"I totally agree, Phillipa, but we are not trying to

run away from her," Letty panted and was rewarded by her companion's instant adoption of a pace more suited to a stroll in the Park as an apology.

The hateful luncheon was over and they had been set down by Lady Mickleham at the Park, where they could both see and be seen by most of the Polite World during the hours of the Promenade. Already they had been nodded to from at least half a dozen carriages and at least that many parties afoot, but no one would accost a young lady going the pace that Phillipa had taken, nor one with such a scowl.

"I can't help it, Letty. She's just so dreadful and I don't see why she gets such pleasure from needling you when she is such a bosom bow of your mother. 'So devoted'!" Her mockery was vicious but accurate.

"You do not know my mother well, Phillipa. After my refusal of the duke, she would have been very happy if I had stayed at Coombs Farm. It was only at Father's threatening to cut off her allowance that she brought me to London for a Season the first time. Poor Mother. It must be difficult to be a reigning beauty when one has an unmarried daugher in her third Season."

"You are kinder to her than I."

"Had it not been for dear Lady Mickleham, I should not be in Town now. Mother never would have allowed me to return."

Phillipa ignored the pain that lately plagued her whenever affairs of the heart were mentioned and smiled at her friend. "From what I've seen, your mother will not be the one who gives instruction to you much longer."

"Why, whatever do you mean?" Letty's question was

most decorous, but the rising flush that covered her face belied her words.

"My dear, I am neither blind nor stupid. I saw the reaction between you and Ronnie as it happened. I think it is wonderful."

"Do you mind?" Letty nodded civilly to Lady Cowper and nudged Phillipa to do the same.

"Mind? Oh, Letty, I think it is wonderful! I love Ronnie dearly and you are the best wife I could think of for him . . . and we shall truly be cousins."

Letty looked at her friend's face, satisfied that her words were genuine, yet still there was something indefinable under them. "Thank you, Phillipa. I wish I could be assured that your aunt felt the same. I know she had hopes for you and Lord Ronald . . ."

"Oh, that was just a passing fancy. She doesn't really want me as a daughter-in-law. You would be much more to her taste. It's just that Aunt Beatrice cannot like anything unless it was her idea first. Doubtless she will figure out some way for her to bring the two of you together and claim all the credit."

"Oh, I hope so. And I wish you could find someone to be happy with."

"I have heard that Sir Rupert Longstreet is returning to Town and will press his suit once more," Phillipa said in a queer voice.

"Phillipa, you couldn't!"

"He is going to be an earl and has a plentiful fortune. I probably shan't get a better offer. Remember, I too am in my third season."

"But you called him a horse-mad sapskull only last year!"

171

"Things have changed since last year, Letty," Phillipa replied repressively. "I think that Longstreet and I could contrive to rub along well enough. As Aunt Beatrice has been at considerable pains to remind me, I am in grave danger of becoming an ape-leader."

"Nonsense! You could have any man you wished."

Phillipa seemed about to say something, but instead stopped to make a most minute examination of a lingering blossom. When her face lifted, her voice was almost under control. "Longstreet will do very well for me, Letty."

There was the whir of wheels and a smart phaeton pulled to a stop. Letty looked up into the face of a man she had never seen before, yet who looked oddly familiar. Dark of hair and with a scowling visage, he was watching them with eyes narrowed to suspicious slits. Obviously he was a gentleman, but such a strange, dour one! Letty turned quickly to Phillipa, as she was accustomed to do, and was treated to a rare sampling of emotion flitting across her friend's face. Letty's intellectual powers were not great, but it would not take a mental giant to connect this dark, scowling man with the man who had figured so prominently in Phillipa's delirium. On the other hand, if this were he, why were they not rushing at each other in joyful reunion?

"Good afternoon," he said to Phillipa. "Will you join me?"

"I cannot, for I fear I cannot leave my friend alone." Phillipa trembled with what might have been indignation. How dare he stop and speak to her in the Park, where anyone might see?

"At least you could introduce us."

Phillipa hesitated long enough for him to realize it was a futile request. Being a gentleman, he sketched a bow in Letty's direction, but his eyes never left Phillipa's face.

Making decisions was obviously becoming a habit with Letty, for she made one very quickly and said, "Nonsense, Phillipa. There's no reason you shouldn't enjoy a ride in this lovely phaeton. Pray don't decline on my account, for there is dear Mrs. Chaney and her daughter and I'm sure they would have no objection to my joining their party while you're gone. But I must hurry if I am going to catch them, for they are turning onto the Long Walk now . . . sir . . ."

"How very charitable of your friend. Now you can climb up."

Phillipa looked up into the dark face. She should hate herself for going weak in the knees. "I have no intention of going anywhere with you."

"Perhaps not, but we must talk and this is the way it must be done. Now, are you getting up, or must I come down and abduct you forcibly?"

"You dare!"

"Do you doubt me?"

For one small moment Phillipa considered screaming, for she had not the slightest worry that he would hesitate to carry out his threat, but that would only bring undue attention upon herself, which she could ill afford at this moment. It was common practice to take a turn around the Park during the Promenade and would certainly cause less talk than to resist violently. She accepted his outstretched hand and climbed into the phaeton, settling as far from him as the narrow seat would allow.

173

"I'm not going to bite you."

"I have no assurance of that." She stared doggedly ahead, impressed, against her will, by his blooded matched grays and the way he handled them. "After what I saw at Saint Gregory's, I do not think a person of your caliber very trustworthy in even the most minor matter."

To her absolute fury, he began to chuckle. "You think my biting you is a minor matter? No, no, don't rage at me again. I commend your tactics. First stroke is to attack me as if I were the guilty party. . . . Masterly."

"*As if!*" Phillipa said, seething, but forced herself to nod cordially to a party in a passing barouche. "I will not stay in this carriage—"

"It's a phaeton," he corrected with maddening calm.

"I will not stay one moment more! Not one! Be so kind as to put me down this instant."

"Not until we have had our talk," Geraint said with authority, snapping the horses into a smart trot.

Phillipa considered the wisdom of leaping from the vehicle, but despite the distinct possibility of physical injury, there was the certainty of unwanted interest, so she forced herself to sit proudly and look out over the Park with a semblance of equanimity.

"You might smile. I should hate to have people mistake my poor phaeton for a tumbrel. People might remark on it."

Several scathing retorts occurred to Phillipa, but unfortunately so did the wisdom of his remark, so she contented herself with turning on him a dazzling smile. Only he was close enough to see the frigid blaze in her eyes. Neither of them noticed a stolid figure in brown watching them from the road with every evidence of intense interest. Unaware of the close scrutiny to which they were being subjected, the pair drove on, out of the young man's sight, a great deal more unconcerned about everything save each other than they should be.

The sober figure in brown was not the only interested observer of the spectacle the pair presented. A great number of casual onlookers merely commented on a nice pairing of two very good-looking young members of the ton, but two pairs of eyes fastened on the silent couple with varying degrees of disapproval.

"Shameless creature," Eustacia, Duchess of Connaught, murmured as if she would never dream of riding beside Paul Ludlowe herself. "Flinging herself on the man like that."

Honoria Valelyn nodded and made agreeable noises. Realizing the value of her new friend and protector, she knew the wisdom of maintaining a similar train of thought, but as this time she had an equal score to settle with the unfortunate Miss Stanhope-Fredericks, her agreements carried a weight and sincerity they had not always had before. "It's a miracle that she's still received," Honoria said quietly. "I still haven't been able to get the full story, but there was definitely something havey-cavey about her illness this spring."

Their eyes met in perfect amity. "How dear of you to remind me, sweetest Honoria. We cannot be too careful in the vigilance we maintain toward the respectability of our set, can we? We must redouble our efforts to do our duty toward protecting our young ones," Eustacia purred.

A third pair of eyes watching was also displeased to see Miss Stanhope-Fredericks a passenger in Lord Ludlowe's phaeton, but for entirely different reasons. Sir Rupert Longstreet was a cautious man, but once his mind was made up, the decisions were unalterable. After long deliberation he had decided that Miss Stanhope-Fredericks was the only gently bred female of his acquaintance with whom he could foresee the possibility of a tolerably happy life together—not a little influenced by the fact that his benefactor stood able to bestow upon him much more than the title alone if he married suitably, and Arkwright had been a great admirer of Miss Stanhope-Fredericks's late uncle, Lord George Mickleham. Despite the fact that he had not yet been accepted by the lady in question, due to the sad death of her younger brother, he regarded her as his own, for what young woman of sensibility could turn down a sober personage of wealth and a potential earl? Out of feelings of delicacy for her recently discarded state of mourning and her seemingly precarious health—for all of London had heard of her lengthy illness that spring—he had not yet renewed his suit. Even so, Longstreet was confident of the outcome until he saw her sitting as big as life with that rake Ludlowe and not even in a respectable carriage, but in a rather dashing phaeton. Surely all London rang with gossip about Ludlowe's exploits in the field of battle and espionage, but that was by no means all that was needed to make him respectable enough to drive out with Sir Rupert Longstreet's almost betrothed.

Some might consider Longstreet a slow and careful

man, but no one could question his courage. He nudged his horse into a trot and pulled alongside the carriage, nodding to the occupants.

Ludlowe groaned inwardly. First icy stares from Eustacia Winterthorpe and now this country bumpkin. It would almost seem that the Fates themselves were bent on protecting this girl, preventing his even talking to her. Phillipa had much the same line of thought regarding her situation. Sir Rupert was far removed from the accepted vision of a divine messenger, but she was grateful enough for any distraction to give him a wide smile of welcome.

"Servant," Longstreet said civilly, sketching a bow in Ludlowe's direction while focusing all his attention on Phillipa. "I had to see if this was really you, up and about and looking so well."

"You are too kind, sir," Phillipa murmured.

"I had heard that you were returned to Town," Sir Rupert went on, impervious to Ludlowe's glares.

"Yes, just a few days ago." Phillipa's mind was working at a frantic speed. Not even the notoriously thick-skinned Sir Rupert could be unaware of Geraint's rising annoyance much longer.

Fortune smiled on Phillipa, for among the promenaders she saw a lady who had made her come-out the same year and had married not long after. "There's Cecily Lane-Harris! I had no idea she'd returned to Town." Phillipa turned to Catton with a tight, civil smile. "I know this is dreadfully shocking and rude, but I really must speak to her. I'm sure you understand. Sir Rupert, would you be so kind as to help me dismount?"

Always polite, Longstreet was also aware that from his point of view Mrs. Lane-Harris was a much more suitable companion for his about-to-be-betrothed than the dashing hero of the Peninsular Wars, so he obeyed his chosen lady's commands, dismounting his own horse with alacrity and handing Miss Stanhope-Fredericks down with the greatest of care.

"I look forward to continuing our little conversation soon, ma'am," Ludlowe said through a suspiciously rigid jaw. "Your servant."

The retreating phaeton was watched with relief by both Sir Rupert and Miss Stanhope-Fredericks, though for totally different reasons. Almost shaking from fear and suppressed, despised emotion, Phillipa was grateful for Longstreet's stolid, benign presence. Perhaps he did not make her pulse race and her emotions take wing as did the wicked man to whom she had unwillingly given heart, but with him she would be safe—and bored, she had to admit. Longstreet would protect her and give her a solid life. It was not to be despised.

"Frippery fellow," Longstreet snorted, unaware of how favorably his suit had progressed in the last moments. "Can't think how you could come to associate with a man like that." He was still unhappy at seeing the lady he had chosen for himself being annoyed by a rakish creature such as Ludlowe and wished sincerely for the authority to order him away. Although things were undoubtedly settled between Miss Stanhope-Fredericks and himself—after all, she had known of his intentions before the tragedy had stricken her family—the sooner they got the formalities over with the better.

"Might I find you at home tomorrow, Miss Stanhope-Fredericks? I should like to pay my respects to your honored mother and lady aunt and formally bid you all welcome back to Town."

"Oh, dear, we do seem to be at cross-purposes! I am so sorry, but my aunt has engaged a shopping spree tomorrow. She swears every garment I own is so outmoded as to make her a laughingstock. However, we shall be at Almack's tomorrow night and"—Phillipa made a heroic effort not to cry as she calmly and finally accepted her fate—"I shall endeavor to be at home the following afternoon, if you would care to call then."

Longstreet smiled. It was not as soon as he had hoped, but he did understand the importance women put on clothes and fripperies and such, funny little creatures that they were. Still, Miss Stanhope-Fredericks's invitation gave him every reason to hope that the necessities could be taken care of speedily and then he could return to his lands and quit worrying about silly socialites. It was with great good humor then that he relinquished the companionship of his almost-betrothed into the keeping of Mrs. Lane-Harris and after a few hearty compliments watched them walk away into the Park, chatting artlessly as he knew women did when they were happy and untroubled.

CHAPTER TWENTY-ONE

The owner of the Bell Tavern was a taciturn man, quite prudently so, as his establishment was in an unwholesome part of town and frequented by people whom it would be better not to cross. He had a fair idea of the nature of the deals that were discussed over his scarred tables, but there were some things it was safer to know nothing about. At one time the Bell had been a respectable coaching inn, but then times had changed and it had sunk to its present low estate. Just once had Eli Latham hoped to raise the Bell to a higher status again, but his patrons had forcibly objected, fearing to lose their safe gathering place, so he had resigned himself to always running a hedge tavern of smoky repute. The Bell had remained the same, which made the arrival of the stranger that much more curious.

The stranger had been a topic of conversation ever since his arrival in the night some days before. There had been a steady drizzle falling all day, filling the taproom almost to capacity with the regular customers, who were lured by a stout roof, good ale, and a roaring fire. The heat of the blaze combined with the damp clothing worn by the unwashed men and the thick scent of good home-brewed ale to form a steamy, heady atmosphere that would have daunted a number of men not used to its potent aroma.

He had come into the dim taproom directly, for the Bell was an old place and did not boast a hall, shaking drops of moisture from his cloak and glancing about the crowded room with a wary eye. His stocky, muscular body was clothed in a suit of sturdy brown wool and only slightly yellowed linen trimmed with one thin row of lace, a perfect example of a North Country merchant's son come to London to see the sights.

In the ensuing days both Eli and some of his regular customers had tried to find out something about their visitor—each for his own reasons—but while maintaining a distant courtesy, the young man had managed to give away no information worth knowing. He left the inn every morning and stayed gone until time for supper, regular as the tide, making no trouble and speaking to no one. Eventually the other patrons seemed to accept him and he ceased to be an object of comment, which suited Seth just fine.

It had been a long and twisting road from the burning ruin of St. Gregory's to the Bell Tavern on the outskirts of London, a time of running and hiding, of never being sure if he were about to be captured or not. During that time Seth had learned both the wary silence of the hunted and the invaluable knack of blending into the background. His travels had taken him through many places and many names, but always pointing toward London. He had been right to come to London. There were so many opportunities here for a bright young man with a lot of brains and not many scruples. Seth already knew quite a lot. He had chosen the Bell Tavern because of the quality of its customers, for the safest place for a hunted man is among other hunted men. From here he could look around and plan his next move.

It had been so easy; simply a new name—Mr. Pascoe—and a secondhand suit of clothes and, there! He was a whole, new person. Already he had sufficient, if superficial, manners and decorum to carry off the impersonation, having assiduously studied the masters at St. Gregory's, especially the last history master—the one who had carried that pretty kitchen wench out just as the building was collapsing. Damn fool thing to do, Seth thought, even though that particular act of heroism did distract everyone so that he could make good his own escape. He smiled meditatively. Admittedly the chit had been a rare looker, but hardly worth risking one's life for!

They had made a pretty pair in the Park that afternoon, riding past in a phaeton as if they had both been born to the gentry. The sight of the two of them had confirmed a suspicion Seth had long cherished—that they had engineered the raid on St. Gregory's, for they were the only ones—besides himself and old Snodgress, who had burned to a crisp and gotten the death the old devil so richly deserved—who had not been captured by the authorities. It had not taken a great intellect to conjecture that they had taken the money and skipped, and the sight of them this afternoon on only his fourth day in London seemed to confirm his suspicions. In a queer way he admired them, for such impudent daring could only commend itself to him. Indeed, had he been able to think of such an impressive plan on his own, he would have followed it without compunction.

Now his problem was multiplied. They not only had the money, but also a seemingly secure place in Society, which would make approaching them that much more difficult. Conversely, they would be made much more vulnerable by the need to protect that social position and Seth would not have been a true pupil of Mr. Ira Snodgress if he could not turn someone else's weakness to his advantage.

After due consideration Seth smiled, sent for the poor pen and paper that the Bell afforded, hardly having an overly literate clientele, and began to write two notes, which he would keep in his pocket until they were needed; the time was not yet right, but when it was he would want them near. Now he needed an ally, for being but one man he could not be in two places at the same time. Donning his coat and hat once more, he walked out into the deepening dusk, wearing an expression that made Eli Latham speculate on his lodger's good fortune and the wisdom of raising his rates.

Letty tried to make herself small in the corner of the carriage, endeavoring to draw as little attention to herself as possible. Even Lady Mickleham seemed remote and withdrawn, unwilling to break the tight silence. Lord Ronald, though a fearless and noble fighter on the field of warfare, knew his limitations whenever a familial storm was brewing, and had disappeared the night before.

Phillipa was in a mood, and knowing the discomfort

183

it caused her family did not help her dispel it, try though she might. At the musicale the previous evening she had been barely civil, drawing a beautifully raised eyebrow from Sally Jersey, and on returning home she had indulged in a hearty fit of unfamiliar tears. Letty had fretted that her friend was sickening for something, that the Season was too much for her newly recovered and fragile health, but Lady Mickleham had taken the strong line, just as she would have with a nursery tantrum—which, to be fair, it did resemble—and bracingly ordered Phillipa to behave herself, an action which merely precipitated that young lady's flight to her room, where she remained until her pale and silent appearance at breakfast the next morning. Beatrice was more than glad that her sister's fragile health had kept her in the country, for Heaven knows what Arabella would think of her daughter's behavior. Phillipa's unnatural calm—in a way more unsettling than her outbursts of temper—prevailed through the meal and the tiresome ride to Madame Berthe's.

The foremost modiste in Town, Madame Berthe knew her power and used it wisely to build up a carriage trade that was unassailable. Her taste was impeccable, her temper legendary, and the fashionable ladies of London fought for the privilege of being dressed by this genius of thread and lace. Whatever Madame Berthe's volatile French chatter decreed, the ladies wore, whether it suited them or not, secure in the knowledge that nothing by Berthe could be wrong. This fact doubtless accounted for some of the more bizarre outfits that appeared during the Season.

Beatrice Mickleham had been one of the original customers of Madame Berthe, before the addition of the French accent and excitable temperament, when she had been merely a cockney seamstress named Rose Coughlin, who had an exceptional gift with the needle. The young Lady Mickleham had recognized this treasure and was thereafter dressed only by Madame Berthe; it had been a satisfactory arrangement for both parties and a friendship of sorts had grown up over the years.

It was this concern for an old and honored friend that made Madame Berthe break an equally old and honored rule—that all customers should wait on her— by standing in the doorway, waiting for Lady Mickleham to alight from her carriage. She saw the direct cut that Mrs. Wilberforce gave to Miss Stanhope-Fredericks and the shock and indignation on her ladyship's face. Why did they have to come now, and why of all people did they have to meet Mrs. Wilberforce, who was such a starched-up old cat merely because her grandfather had been a favorite of old George II, and who was perhaps the only person in London without any sense of humor at all?

"My dear Lady Mickleham . . ."

Beatrice, in high fettle, was an awe-inspiring sight; suffused with rage, she was enough to make battle-hardened men think twice about crossing her. "Berthe, did you see what that Friday-faced creature did? Exactly who does she think she is, aside from the granddaughter of a man who used to tag after the old king's father like a puppy?"

"I must talk to you, my lady. If the young ladies will go on into the fitting room, Mademoiselle Francine will be happy to help Lady Winterthorpe with the final fitting on the blue satin. Oh, it is *ravissant!*

And, if the young Mademoiselle Stanhope-Fredericks will be so kind as to wait until I can come to her, we will see how she likes her green ball gown. I have named it especially *vert de la mer du sud* . . . *Alors*, mesdemoiselles, if you will just go that way, and my lady, I would so much like a private word with you, if you permit, in my office. . . ." Madame Berthe's voice was carrying enough to be heard throughout the entire shop, for she knew the fitting room walls were thin and that there were customers just waiting to hear what Lady Mickleham would say next. Only the modiste's thickened and highly variable French accent showed the extent of her emotional agitation. Her gestures in escorting Lady Mickleham into her private office would have done justice to a queen born and bred.

Beatrice Mickleham settled into a chair and eyed the sturdy black-clad woman before her. "Berthe, what's going on?"

"I don't know, my lady, save that the Duchess of Connaught and that mushroom friend of hers—"

"Valelyn."

"Yes, that was her name, and a nastier piece of work I've not set eyes on in a year or more. Anyway, they were in today; the duchess made it a point to speak to everyone, real friendly like—"

"Eustacia Winterthorpe? Friendly?"

Berthe nodded. "Yes. She and that Valelyn woman were talking about Miss Stanhope-Fredericks, but then they saw me and hushed. I don't know what's afoot, but the shop was like a beehive after they left. There's no one thing that I can pin down, but something is up."

186

"Thank you, Berthe. I just wish I knew what that she-devil was plotting," Beatrice muttered and didn't bother to apologize for the unladylike description of the Duchess of Connaught. "Now, we'd best not leave the girls alone much longer. I have a feeling this is only starting."

Lady Mickleham's fear of the girls' indiscretion was unfounded, for both young ladies knew of the thinness of the fitting room walls and had confined their remarks exclusively to the pale-blue satin gown topped with ethereal gray sarcanet and studded with bunches of sapphire ribbons that now decorated Lady Lettice's slender form with glorious perfection. Phillipa, her mood darkened by the ugly incident outside, said little save to echo her friend's raptures, her mind occupied by the immediate future and the consequences of her next actions.

Of course, to a young woman of good family there was no choice; Sir Rupert Longstreet was a catch and she would be mad to prefer an obvious adventurer to a future earl. Besides, she had an obligation to her family to marry well. Longstreet was an excellent manager and now that Arnold was dead the whole of her father's property would come to her and her husband, which made the correct decision all the more imperative.

Phillipa's gloomy train of thought was banished by the voluble entrance of Madame Berthe, followed by a flock of underlings bearing the soft green gown and the necessary pins, measures, and scissors like holy objects. Madame proclaimed that the honor of fitting Miss Stanhope-Fredericks was to be hers alone and promptly banished everyone save the ladies Mickleham and Winterthorpe. A compassionate woman in her private life, Madame was distressed by the ugly puckers and weals on Phillipa's shoulder and had gladly undertaken the challenge of designing fashionable gowns to conceal them. The new green dress was a triumph of pale silk with an overdress of darker gauze trimmed with a ransom of rare ivory lace.

Fit for a countess, Phillipa thought, and tried to ignore the small stubborn pain around her heart.

Madame adjusted a small headdress of jeweled feathers, dainty and close to the brow, and clapping her hands like a child, Letty exclaimed, "Phillipa! How utterly beautiful! Every head in Almack's will turn when you come in tonight."

CHAPTER TWENTY-TWO

Letty's prophecy did turn out to be accurate, though not through the agency of either dress or head ornament. From their first steps through the door, the three ladies were aware of a variety of reactions to their presence, ranging from curiosity to withdrawal.

Beatrice, Lady Mickleham, stopped and metaphorically sniffed the social air like the old campaigner she was. Yes, something was most definitely up and she intended to get to the bottom of it. Beside her, the two girls stiffened, still unaccustomed to the rigors of participation in such social infighting.

"Looks like your mother and her creature, Valelyn, have been quite busy," Beatrice whispered. "Courage, my pets. We shall soon see what this is all about. Hold your heads high and act naturally. Never let them see that you think anything is out of the ordinary."

Like a majestic swan with two glorious cygnets, Beatrice sailed across the floor, her face a study of unconcern as she smiled and nodded to her friends. A small ripple of silence followed their progress, which in turn was followed by a counterpoint of sound, whispers punctuated with the rattle of fans and the sharpening of tongues.

Though by no means a soldier, Beatrice realized the wisdom of a strong position and led her charges directly to the dowagers' dais. With a touch of relief she noted that none of the patronesses gave them the cut outright, but then of course those ladies had known the Duchess of Connaught for a number of years and also, to Lady Mickleham's personal knowledge, had watched that lady have affairs with their respective husbands. No, the patronesses of Almack's would not credit Eustacia Winterthorpe's word against that of Beatrice Mickleham without a great deal of solid proof. The only problem was, Beatrice thought, what have Eustacia and that Valelyn harpy been spreading around and how close to the truth was it? As soon as the girls were settled, she would find out.

Mrs. Drummond-Burrell, well known as the stuffiest of the patronesses, studied Phillipa with a cool eye.

"A lovely gown, my dear. You should always wear green."

Phillipa muttered appropriate thanks.

"How delightful and rare it is these days to find a girl who actually prefers to wear a decent neckline instead of those incredible décolletages."

Beatrice thought her heart would stop, for surely she could not hit so close without knowing something. Mrs. Drummond-Burrell was one of the few women in Town who could ruin them utterly and completely. Phillipa was made of stern stuff, however, and her smile did not change; besides, after facing Ira Snodgress in a murderous mood, Mrs. Drummond-Burrell was nothing.

"I merely prefer to set fashions, rather than follow them, ma'am," Miss Stanhope-Fredericks replied sweetly.

"And very commendable too, my dear," said Lady Jersey. As usual she and Mrs. Drummond-Burrell were feuding and anything the elder lady questioned Lady Sally Jersey immediately championed. "Did Berthe make that stunning outfit? I should have known. Absolutely no one has that woman's touch. Ah, but what are you doing here talking with old crones like us?" she asked, her lovely face alight with the joke. With the ease of long practice she introduced Phillipa and Letty to two young men and sent them spinning off across the dance floor. For a fleeting moment Lady Jersey's eyes reflected a kind of envy of the young people waltzing around the floor. Abruptly she turned to Beatrice and the envy turned to curiosity ill-disguised as helpfulness.

"Your pretty niece does look exceptionally well tonight. What a pity she has acquired such powerful enemies. What on earth has she done to offend the Duchess of Connaught?"

"Has she been spreading tales about Phillipa?"

Lady Jersey laughed. "You've still got that devilish trick you learned from that diplomat husband of yours of answering one question with another. Yes, she's been busy as a bee, beating her breast about the fact that her daughter is living with you and how it is making her the laughingstock of Town."

"Of course she treated the girl so well."

"But she is the child's mother—whatever that means. Lady Lettice has veritably blossomed this Season. Is there any truth to the rumor that your good-looking son is trying to fix his interest with her?" Ever avid for a new item of gossip, Lady Jersey fixed her companion with a steady eye.

Lady Mickleham managed a small smile. "He regards her much as he does his cousin Phillipa. He is not such a fool as to wish an alliance with that family! Did our dear duchess talk to you about Phillipa, by the way? I own I am curious what sort of foolishness she is spreading about."

"As nearly as I could tell, not much of anything . . . just a sad lot of innuendo about her illness this spring. The sort of thing that always sounds so damning but can't be pinned to any specific fact. Any truth in it?"

Lady Mickleham drew herself up to her most imperious haughtiness. "My niece? Really, Sally!"

Later, though, watching the unusual phenomenon of Phillipa sitting out three dances in a row and the almost imperceptible flow of conversation about her—

the turning of heads, followed by quick whispers—going around the rooms, Beatrice wondered just exactly how much the Duchess of Connaught and that disgusting Valelyn woman knew and what they were telling. Innuendo, but without solid fact, Sally Jersey had said; the easiest kind to spread and the hardest to stop. Many reputations less shaky than Phillipa's had been ruined because of less. Thunderation, why was she saddled with such a creature? Why couldn't Phillipa have been a nice docile girl like Letty?

Her ladyship was pleasantly pulled out of her melancholy humor a few moments later to see that her niece, her own humor unimproved by the novel sensation of being ignored so pointedly and exquisitely, was being approached by a very good-looking man. A trifle dark for her ladyship's taste, he was still handsome enough in a rough-hewn sort of way to rouse a flurry of feeling in a maiden's breast.

It was just as well that Lady Mickleham was ignorant of the exact nature of the emotions that flared to life in Phillipa as she identified the gentleman, for such contradictions and intensities would have been highly distressing to the older lady. Recognition, shock, anger, and a quick, shimmering flicker of passion raced through Miss Stanhope-Fredericks in a rapid swirl. What a pity she was constrained to sit here and watch that loathesome man advance as if he had a right to be here, of all places, at Almack's! For once in her life she regretted the absence of a crowd of people into which she could make a polite and graceful escape, or a dull, safe young man to which she could appeal for a dance. Now, with the strange mood that the crowd held against her tonight, she had no one and was well and truly trapped. Centuries of breeding and a fortune in governess's fees seemed to be utterly wasted as her face took on a distinctly unsocial, mulish look, and she prepared for battle.

Brought to the sacred portals of the Marriage Mart by his half-hearted intentions of finding a suitable wife, Ludlowe had been watching Phillipa for a few minutes and, after his initial surprise at finding her at Almack's, felt a queer kind of pity for her. Her admittance here had been a masterly triumph of social maneuvering, but she was surely getting the cold shoulder now. A perverse kind of compassion—not to mention a strong desire to hold her in his arms once more, no matter the cost to his injured leg—sent him across the room to her, and he smiled at the change in her face on recognizing him. He knew and understood that look. Once he had rescued a small kitten from a watery death and in its terror the tiny soaked bundle of fur had turned on him with fierce teeth and claws.

"As you seem to be unattached, might I have this dance? I assume that with your other attainments you have the permission of the patronesses to waltz?"

Phillipa looked up into his lean features and was wrenched by a painful mixture of disgust and desire. "Of course I have permission, but I prefer to sit this one out."

"I think not, my fine lady. You seem to be making enough of a spectacle of yourself sitting here alone without compounding it by turning down a very civil invitation."

"Civil!" was Phillipa's only rejoinder, as she reluctantly saw the logic of his words. There was nothing for it, she would have to dance with the man, for at least four of the dowagers were looking on with interest and a sprinkling of curious glances flashed at them from the dance floor.

"Good girl. Come along." With an ease that belied both his wound and long absence from the social forms, he swept her out onto the floor. Whatever pain there was in his leg was overridden, obliterated by the sheer physical joy of holding her in his arms again, of smelling the fresh scent of her hair, of the pure physical contact of his flesh against hers.

Like a vibration, the same emotions passed through Phillipa's mind, and for the few moments her conscience would allow, her treacherous heart forgot everything save the physical pleasure of the nearness of him. "Won't dancing hurt your leg?"

"How conscientious of you! As a matter of fact, it hurts like the devil, but as the music is ending now, I think I managed very well. Do I detect concern on your face? Good Heavens, don't look like that. We shall both be disgraced if anyone sees you burst out weeping."

Phillipa looked up fiercely. "I have no intention of weeping, here or anywhere else."

He studied her upturned face intensely. "No, I don't think you would. We've got to talk, you know."

"We have nothing to say."

"Now you know that isn't true, my dear."

"And I am not your dear," Phillipa said in a tone that was a trifle too loud.

"Such fury. Almack's surely dislikes such open displays of emotion."

"How can you be so sure? I have not seen you here before. They seem to have lowered their standards shockingly tonight." Phillipa's tone was scathing and her anger was increased by the fact that he seemed to be amused.

"I must acknowledge a hit. Again you prove the wisdom of a good attack." With outwardly exquisite courtesy, he handed her back to her lonely seat, and only she knew that his firm grip on her hand was not that of a suitor. "We will talk, you know. There are things that must be said."

"I have nothing to say to you," she said woodenly.

"But I have a great deal to say to you," he replied and then was gone to be seen no more that night. His conflicting emotions needed to be sorted out and disciplined, a process that was too deep to be done in the glare of social life.

Phillipa danced again several times and sat out several more dances with Letty, who through the dint of long experience was more accustomed to a sideline experience. At first Letty was somewhat fearful, knowing her friend's pride and temper—a fearsome combination, especially to the timid—and waited for a scene that would be their final disgrace. To Lady Lettice's relief, however, Phillipa was distracted and silent, even more so after her dance with the dark man from the Park. Letty had hoped that after that dance Phillipa's mood would be lightened, but it had only darkened, leaving Letty quite confused.

It was almost the magic hour of eleven, after which no one was to be admitted, when Letty looked up and then dug an excited elbow into her companion's unsuspecting ribs.

"Letty! What on earth . . . ?"

"Look!"

Phillipa followed her friend's look and gasped. Sir Rupert had said something about seeing her at Almack's, but she had really not expected to have that sturdy countryman truly invade the portals of such a frivolous place. Even Phillipa's active mind was boggled by the incredible sight coming toward them, though she was too polite to laugh, even inwardly.

Longstreet in country riding clothes was an impressive figure, a man in his own place; even in Town clothes he was to be respected, though obviously out of his element. In the knee breeches and silk hose required by Almack's, he was ludicrous, just like a sturdy plowhorse decked out in festival ribbons and flowers, Phillipa thought. And this man bid fair to be her future husband!

That melancholy thought stayed with her all through the rest of the interminable evening while Sir Rupert punctiliously paid her every proper attention under the approving eyes of the dowagers, through her long and sleepless night and well into the morning as she dragged herself down to the breakfast room. In a way it was very lucky that Longstreet was such a country mouse, she thought morosely, for then he would not mind that his wife was no longer of the first stare of Society. She could bury herself in the country and raise her children, oversee the stillrooms and the gardens . . . Such visions of a highly probable future were so depressing that she could barely choke down what the others considered a delicious breakfast.

Lady Mickleham took one look at her niece, pronounced that she was sickening from something, and forbade her to leave the house that afternoon. They were engaged to an opera outing that night and Phillipa was to spend her time resting. Meekly Phillipa agreed and gladly saw her aunt and her friends off on their rounds of calls and shopping. She had been searching for an excuse to stay home and now it had been given to her. She had told no one of Longstreet's proposed visit this afternoon, nor of its purpose, having always preferred to face her fences alone. It would be easier to present Aunt Beatrice with a fait accompli than to have to endure her well-intended but heavy-handed meddling. Time after time her aunt had told her that a girl's responsibility to her family was to marry well.

Well, Phillipa thought, she couldn't do much better than Longstreet. The sooner the thing was done the better. With leaden feet and a heart to match, she went into the garden for a breath of air. There were at least three hours that had to be filled before Longstreet could decently be expected to call, and the garden always had a soothing effect on her, as well as making her homesick for Worthington Grange. Perhaps a future of being immured in the country was not to be so despised.

The wind was unexpectedly cold; Phillipa went into the scullery for the heavy cloak that always hung there. It belonged to one of the maids, kept handy for errands in inclement weather, but Phillipa did not wish to trouble about sending for one of her own. There was something so real and solid about the coarse, heavy wool that seemed an effective counterbalance against the fantastic instability her world had acquired since Arnold's death.

Perhaps marriage to Longstreet would be the best thing for her. He was kind and maybe in time she would come to love him. Certainly she had nothing against him—except that he wasn't Geraint Catton—and many successful marriages had started with less. She did enjoy living in the country, and it was said that Crowther Hall was beautiful.

The stone, wrapped in paper, landed right at Phillipa's feet, startling her from her reverie. For a few moments she stared stupidly at it, then, roundly berating herself for being a timid ninnyhammer, she picked it up and read the note, which had been hastily scrawled on rude paper with a dull pencil.

I must see you. About St. Gregory's. The back garden gate in one hour.

A quick glance up and down the street showed nothing but a sober tradesman some houses away, secure and stolid in dark brown. There was no tall, muscular figure with a lean face and dark hair to be seen. But then, Phillipa thought, he might have even used an errand boy or some such. The arrogance of the man, not even requesting an answer, just assuming her compliance. For a few headstrong moments she considered his consternation if she did not answer the summons, but logic finally won. He was right in that they had to talk, and if she refused this time, he might force it on her in a more public place. No, there had to be a final confrontation and this was as good a time as any. Maybe this time she could rid her heart of that man once and for all. With an air of one about to do a distasteful task, Phillipa shoved the note into her pocket and settled in a part of the garden somewhat protected from the chilly winds.

198

Precisely at the hour, she stood by the back gate, which opened on the small side street that led to the mews, and was rewarded by the sound of a jingling harness. Vainly Miss Stanhope-Fredericks tried to attribute her quickened pulse and rapid breath to the prolonged stay in the garden's chilly air, but as her hands fumbled with the gate latch she knew herself a liar. He would be standing there . . .

Phillipa never saw the longed-for face, for the simple reason that as the gate swung open she was enveloped in a swirl of black cloth that was thick and dusty and quickly secured about her midriff with cruel firmness. Strong arms lifted her up into some sort of vehicle, ignoring her limited struggles with an almost insulting disregard. The door slammed behind her, the carriage gave a lurch, and they were moving. She struggled into a sitting position only to fall again as an explosion of lights went off inside her head and she pitched forward into blackness.

CHAPTER TWENTY-THREE

The ladies Mickleham and Winterthorpe returned from a highly satisfactory shopping expedition to find Summerhill waiting for them in the hallway, his usually impassive face agitated.

"Might I speak with you, my lady?" Summerhill asked, and on receiving a nod, went on. "It's about Miss Phillipa."

"What about her?"

"She's nowhere to be found."

"What?"

Summerhill was driven by his mistress's loud tones to make small shushing sounds. "Sir Rupert Longstreet, madam."

"Here?" Lady Mickleham hissed.

"Yes, madam. He called at three, asking to speak to Miss Phillipa. I put him in the drawing room . . ."

"Very proper. Go on."

". . . and then found that Miss Phillipa had gone out apparently, for she was not in the house. I checked with the servants and no one has seen her since breakfast."

Letty's face was pale. What had happened to her friend now? "Did no one think to inquire whether she wanted any luncheon?"

Summerhill looked pained. "Begging your pardon, my lady, but I was aware of how tired and ill she looked at breakfast, so when it was time for luncheon I instructed Loring not to wake her if she were sleeping. Loring knocked on her door but there was no answer, so we thought Miss was resting."

"And she probably wasn't there." Inwardly Beatrice swore with a fluency that would have astonished her son. What on earth had she done to be saddled with a girl like this? "Did Loring check her wardrobe? Are any of her clothes missing?"

"Yes, my lady, Loring did check, but nothing is gone save the costume she was wearing at breakfast.

However, Maud, the underhouse parlor maid, says that her heavy cloak is missing from the scullery."

Beatrice groaned. That girl! If she ever got her hands on her . . . "What have you told Sir Rupert?"

"Nothing, my lady, save that Miss Phillipa was not receiving at the moment. I didn't feel it my place to tell him she was out, since it appears to have been rather clandestine."

Thank Heaven for good servants! Lady Mickleham nodded. "Well done. Is he still here?"

"Yes, my lady. I just this moment left him. He wished me to take another message to Miss Phillipa, stating that it was indeed he, and that he had called as promised and would wait."

"As promised? Does that mean the wretched girl was expecting him?"

"It would seem so, my lady."

Lady Mickleham drew a deep breath. "Very well. We must see what we can salvage of this. Letty, go on up to your room. It will be better if I do this alone. Summerhill, dispatch a footman to find Lord Ronald. Dispatch all of them and the grooms too, if necessary, but find him. I will speak to Sir Rupert."

Longstreet, rising to his feet at the entrance of Lady Mickleham, would never have guessed that anything was wrong from his hostess's gracious greetings or offers of refreshment. He was a little put out over the cavalier message Miss Stanhope-Fredericks had sent down by the butler, especially after her apparent understanding of his offer to call and her sweet behavior the previous evening.

"I am so sorry to have been out when you called, Sir Rupert. How shocking that you should have been left to wait alone," Beatrice purred in her most social tones after they were seated. "Did my niece expect you to call today?"

"Yes, we had set the appointment the day before yesterday."

The sly little minx, Beatrice thought. *If Longstreet hasn't come to fix his interest, I . . . and she said nothing!* "Dear Phillipa did say something about having a caller this afternoon, but we did not know it would be you. The poor dear was in such pain, we did not feel right to question her."

"Pain?"

"Yes, a migraine. . . . She's been overdoing these past days, and I, for one, fear she isn't as recovered from her late illness as she pretends. But the child does hate to worry anyone, especially as her mother is in such fragile health. After Almack's last night we had to bring her straight home to rest. I'm afraid I'm to blame for her being unable to come down today, for since she was unable to sleep, I gave her a good dose of laudanum and left orders she was not to be disturbed."

Longstreet's tender heart was touched. No wonder she had been so quiet the night before. She had been in such pain and had ignored it for the sake of his company. His resentment dropped away and he was filled with warmth toward his chosen bride.

"I understand. Might I be permitted to call tomorrow to inquire about her health?"

Lady Mickleham nodded graciously, but hedged her bets. "Of course. However I feel it only fair to tell you it might be several days before she is strong enough to receive visitors. These attacks are rare, but very debilitating."

"Please tell Miss Stanhope-Fredericks I wish her the very best and will call daily until she feels strong enough to see me. I don't wish to distress her, but . . ." Longstreet's flow of eloquence ran short, but the expression on his face told Beatrice all she wished to know.

After all the proper good-byes and well-wishes for the invalid were said, Beatrice sank into a chair and rested her head on her hands. What a coil! Where was that wretched girl, and what was she doing when she knew Longstreet had come to make her an offer? If only Ronnie would come!

Lord Ronald, however, was amusing himself in a place of which his mother did not know and was, all in all, better off not knowing about, as she held very strong views against cockfighting and bullbaiting, views which obviously clashed with his own. It was only with effort that Ronnie remembered his promise to escort them to the opera that evening, almost as a penance for skipping Almack's the night before. Despite the fact that he had backed a string of winners, his conscience was strong enough to leave the sport, until a friendly hand clapped his shoulder.

"Longstreet!" Lord Ronald saluted his companion with an easy familiarity, despite the fact that, until he had started dangling after Phillipa, they had been the barest of acquaintances. "Didn't think you went in for this sort of thing."

"I'm not a betting man," his lordship admitted, "but Cattermole—there, in the wine-colored waistcoat—is

203

running a string of terriers today. He was my closest friend at Cambridge, and this is the first time he's run his dogs. Been breeding them for years to get just the right temperament."

Ronnie began to like Longstreet a lot more. He might be a stuffy old crock, but anyone who had a friend who raised championship dogs . . . "Done scientifically, eh? Which are his? What's their weight?"

"I don't know their weight, but they're all wearing blue collars. Look, have you any news of your cousin?"

Ronnie's heart skipped a beat. Was Phillipa off on a new lark?

"Pia?"

"Yes. I was by this afternoon, but it wouldn't be the thing to call twice in one day and I thought you might know something more."

"No, I haven't been to my mother's since yesterday . . . I keep my own lodgings, you know. What's the matter with Pia?"

"Migraine. It sounds serious, since your mother dosed her with laudanum to help her sleep." Longstreet managed to make Ronnie sound a monster of inhumanity for being so ignorant of his cousin's condition.

"Well, you can be sure everything's all right if my mother's there to look after her," Ronnie said bracingly and then requested an introduction to the scientific Mr. Cattermole. Deuced shame that Pia was ill, but it gave a fellow a bit of a breather from the social round, and especially the opera. The prospect of an evening of freedom was like a gift, and after the

204

fights he just might ride over and blow a cloud with Ludlowe. If the timing were right, he just might get invited to dinner. Ludlowe kept an excellent chef. Ronnie smiled at the prospect.

CHAPTER TWENTY-FOUR

It was a miserable evening. The persistent drizzle that had started in the late afternoon was trying mightily to turn into snow and the streets were wet and treacherous. Ludlowe stood for a moment, wishing that he could forget the opera—nothing but a bunch of yelling anyway—and sit at home, spending an evening by his own fireside with no company save a bowl of punch and a new book. It was a tempting prospect, but after all, he had given his word to Lord Pendragon to tell him some of the unpublished details regarding the Peninsular campaign, and the opera had seemed a safe enough place in which to do it.

Besides, there was always the opportunity—and Ludlowe would not admit this to anyone, hardly even to himself—of seeing Phillipa again. Strange, he had even come to think of her as Phillipa; it seemed to suit her more than Maggie, though he was surprised at her choosing something so out of the ordinary. She would have been better off with a more feminine, more popular name such as Catherine or Emma or Frances. A smile had touched his lips even as the thought had appeared, for he could not imagine his proud adventuress with any of such undistinguished names. No, Phillipa she would stay.

"The coach is ready, sir." Barton handed Ludlowe his hat and opened the door, letting in a blast of damp air that eddied around the hall, causing Ludlowe's leg to ache painfully. Dancing on it last night had been a damn fool thing to do. Again his mind pictured the comfortable library, a fire roaring in the grate, then he shrugged, nodded to Barton, and stepped out into the rain.

Later he could not remember from where the urchin came, only that one of the sorriest-looking children in all of London suddenly stood before him, so wrapped in filthy rags and tatters that it took a second glance to discern it as a human being rather than a magically animated refuse heap. A scrawny arm emerged from the muffling folds and pointed to Ludlowe.

"Be ye Geraint Catton?"

Ludlowe stiffened. Only a few had ever known him by that name, and only in connection with the affair at St. Gregory's. "I have been called that."

With the quickness of practice the child shoved a grimy letter at Ludlowe and made as if to bolt, but the man was even faster than he and held his arm in a grip that brooked no nonsense.

"No, my boy, not so fast. Who sent this to me?"

Realizing the futility of struggle, the boy stood still, as an animal would, waiting for the chance of escape. "Just a cove, yer honor."

"Barton! Here, hold this creature." Ludlowe thrust the child at his butler. "It's worth your place if he gets away."

Only the vaguest flicker of reaction showed on Barton's properly schooled countenance and he moved forward, loath to touch such an unwholesome specimen, but far too knowledgeable of the temperaments and freaks of his master to even consider declining.

Seeing the child safely held by a disapproving Barton, Ludlowe slipped into the relative protection of the doorway, trying to keep the note from becoming any more waterlogged than it already was. The cheap paper absorbed water quickly, making the pale pencil scrawl difficult to read and the folds desperately fragile. Ludlowe read it twice to make sure he completely understood the meaning.

Catton—I has Maggie. I want my share from St. Gregory's. Send £600 to Mr. Pascoe at General Delivery.

Seth

Ludlowe gritted his teeth and swore, very softly and very thoroughly, then turned to the urchin wearing such a dark expression that the child thought himself confronted by the Devil in person. The urchin struggled, but Barton, mindful of his master's threat, held firm and would probably have given up his next year's salary to see the contents of the note that had sent his lordship into such a temper.

Unmindful of the drizzling rain and his soaked evening clothes, Ludlowe crouched down until his face was on a level with the boy's. "Look here, you little street arab. I need to know who that man is and where I can find him. Now, what is this man's name and where can I find him?"

If Ludlowe had raised his voice, it would have been a different, futile story, for the child had been raised in an atmosphere where shouts and blows were a normal means of communication and were therefore nothing out of the ordinary, but the slow, deliberate speech and intensity of manner were something entirely new and unsettling.

The urchin hesitated. "Pascoe, sur. He was at the Bell Tavern."

"Is that where he's taken the lady?"

Barton tried to look disinterested. A female! He had known it! Never had the master been in such an uncertain temper, now up, now down, for so long. Of course there had to be a woman in the picture. He wondered if Fripping knew anything about this. What a coup for himself if the master's own valet knew nothing!

The urchin's eyes widened. "He's nabbed her? I dunno nothing about that, sur. I dunno where he took her, sur, honest I don't! I was just to watch you and give you that note. Truly, sur—"

"Do be quiet!" Ludlowe ordered without anger, sensing the truth under the child's panic. Phillipa gone, and what was he going to do about it? Of course, it could be a ruse, if she and Seth had been truly working together, but somehow that seemed less and less of a viable possibility. At the school she had seemed afraid of him, it was true, and it had seemed too real to be an act. Also, why the demand for a paltry six-hundred pounds? Even a man of Seth's limited intellect should realize that if she married Ronnie there would be much more than that. No, he had been wrong all along. Whatever game she was playing, Phillipa was playing a lone hand. And Seth had her!

After a moment's furious thought Ludlowe—wearing an expression that would have made some of his battle-hardened former subordinates consider desertion—turned back to the strange pair of proper butler and street arab, both now soaked by the relentless weather. Barton was somewhat used to the distempers of his master, but the child had never before seen such a scowl on a human countenance and, still aware of the painful grip on his shoulder, quietly gave himself up for dead.

Ludlowe's attention was drawn to the waiting coach by the restive movements of his horses; his chestnuts were prime blood stock and loathed to be kept standing. He might wish for the carriage when he found Phillipa, but at the moment Ludlowe's prime concern was speed and mobility, two attributes best found on horseback.

"John! Take the carriage back to the stables. I shan't be needing it tonight. Saddle Thor for me and come back around in ten minutes. I shall need you to carry a note to Lord Pendragon. Barton, send Fripping to me. And don't let that child out of your sight. Not until tomorrow at least."

When Fripping entered his master's chambers some moments later he was thunderstruck to see Lord Ludlowe still wearing the elegant evening dress he had selected earlier, now dripping wet, sitting at the writing desk, unmindful of either the chair or carpet. "My lord! You're drenched. You'll catch your death. . . .

Let me help you out of those wet things and ring for a posset—"

"Nonsense, Fripping. A little wetting never hurt anyone. Lay out my riding clothes—the ones from the country. I'll probably see some hard going tonight. Oh, and find that heavy cloak I brought back from Spain. It'll be the warmest thing." Ludlowe finished his hastily scrawled note, affixed a wafer, then proceeded to divest himself of the wet clothing, throwing it into a corner with a disregard for the fine material that sent shivers up Fripping's back.

Ludlowe was dressed and waiting in the hallway before the appointed ten minutes was up. Thor, his blooded gray, was more restive than usual, having had no exercise the past day, and displeased with being brought out on such a nasty night.

"Watch Thor, sir. He's in a temper this evening," John cautioned, handing over the reins. After one look at the master's face the groom thought that the horse wasn't the only one in a bad humor.

"We'll manage. We've got a lot to do tonight. Here, take this note to Lord Pendragon. He's probably still at home . . . in Cavendish Square." Ludlowe swung lightly into the saddle and, not allowing the restive gray one buck or caper, spurred him into a pace that was sheer madness over the rapidly icing streets.

Ludlowe had a good idea of where the Bell Tavern was; he also had a good idea of its reputation—a haven for wharf rats, cutpurses, scroungers, and worse. Surely Seth wouldn't hold Phillipa there; not even he could expose her to such danger, such an unpredictable element. No, to be sure, Seth would not risk having control taken out of his hands by the professionals at the Bell. Then where? Where? It couldn't be far, Ludlowe reasoned. He couldn't have had Phillipa long, and there was the child with the note . . . but then he could have her anywhere! Anywhere! And Phillipa was with him. She would be terrified, he knew, but she wouldn't show it; she would raise her chin and glare defiantly back, just like at St. Gregory's . . . No, she would never show her fear, Ludlowe thought. He must save her! She must be all right, no matter what she had done, she must be all right! Everything else could be worked out, he decided, but it was not really a recent decision, it was a reality he had been struggling against for days, since he first saw her in the ballroom on Ronnie's arm.

For the past few moments Ludlowe had been vaguely aware of a loud voice, unusual in these quiet streets, and finally one word penetrated his feverish cogitations. That word was "Pablo!"

"What the devil are you doing here?"

Lord Mickleham was taken a bit aback. He reined in his horse, taking care to stay a safe distance from Ludlowe's restive gray. "Pablo! I've been trying to catch you all the way from your house."

A man in love has no scruples. Ludlowe made a quick decision. An ally, an experienced, trusted ally, would be a great asset, and if Phillipa . . . He didn't dare think that far ahead.

Mickleham was still talking. "I came over to blow a cloud with you. The opera party's off tonight—Phillipa has a headache or some such silly thing. I saw you ride off like a courier and have been chasing you ever since. You ride like a lunatic, man! What's afoot?"

So he knew nothing of Phillipa's capture. "It's a private errand, but I would appreciate your help. I can tell you nothing now save it involves the capture of an utterly unprincipled villain who has no right to be alive at this moment, let alone walking about free. We might be able to run him down tonight."

Ronnie's eyes sparkled. Adventure again, and once more with Pablo. "Let's go."

CHAPTER TWENTY-FIVE

It had been a good night at the Bell; Eli could usually count on a profitable evening when the weather was bad and cold. The fire burned brightly and the sweat poured freely down the mullioned windows, sending streams of water down the plastered walls. Eli shivered; this winter seemed colder than others somehow, for his bones ached with the chill—or maybe he was just getting older.

Without warning the babble of the taproom fell off to a thick, sullen silence, the ranks of the regulars closing against an outsider. Eli looked to see the cause of the disturbance and was rewarded with the sight of a gentleman—country dressed, it was sure, but still definitely a gentleman. Probably a traveler from the country come to Town and benighted by the weather, Eli thought, and all but rubbed his hands together. The

Bell was definitely attracting a better class of trade recently and once again his dim dream of running a posh establishment flickered into brief life. If he could but get a recommendation from a few people, get the gentry started coming here . . . He moved forward, a genial smile on his face.

The silence was not unexpected, for Ludlowe had a very good idea of the character of the Bell and his ears were still ringing from Ronnie's protestations that he could not go into such a place alone. Ludlowe, however, had prevailed just as he had so often in Spain, and a very cold and damp Lord Mickleham waited around the corner with the horses, walking them so that they would not take a chill.

Now, sur, how can we help ye? Can I take yer wrap to dry it?"

Startled by such an unctuous greeting, Ludlowe turned to the villainous-looking creature who must be the landlord. Pablo had automatically adopted the character of a slightly drunken skirter, knowing from experience that people of a certain class fear strong personalities but are more tolerant and informative to weakling specimens. Smiling foolishly, Ludlowe stood just a bit off balance. "Thank you, no, my good man. I am waiting for someone."

Noting his guest's vague gaze into the taproom, the landlord spoke hurriedly, knowing the local behavior toward those who looked too often and too long. "Perhaps I can help ye, sur. I ken most of the regulars."

"Oh, that would be nice. . . . And a drop to keep out the cold," he added, noting that the bar, being far from the fire, was nearly deserted. That would be much more to his purposes, as he had no desire to broadcast his reasons any further than necessary.

The landlord poured a tot of neat rum and Ludlowe pulled at it, tasting the fire of the cheap spirit. Still, unpalatable as it was, he had drunk far worse in Spain. He smiled in a vague way and leaned on the bar.

"I know you are a man of discretion, Landlord · . . ."

"True. None could ever say that Eli Latham was a rattlepate."

"Just as my friend told me!"

"Well, to be sure, sur, I do most kindly appreciate yer friend's saying so." Eli Latham positively glowed. Why, it was already happening! Somehow the gentry was beginning to hear of the Bell and it had started almost before he knew he wanted it. Surely such things were wonderful. "Be he the one ye be searching for?"

"Yes, but I don't seem to see him anywhere. You see," Ludlowe leaned forward, speaking conspiratorily, "I'm a bit late. I just stopped in for a drop to keep out the cold, you see, and the time . . . You know how it is." A sudden smile implied that such predicaments were understood only by men of the world such as they.

"Indeed I do, sur. And what be yer friend's name? Perhaps I might be able to help ye." Latham waxed helpful, overwhelmed by such condescension from a real gent. Already he could see the Bell as a place of fashion, frequented by the gentry who came to tipple a noggin or blow a cloud with their genial, respected host.

"Pascoe."

"Oh, sur . . . ye be late indeed. Mr. Pascoe left

early this afternoon. Nigh on to two of the clock, it were."

None of Ludlowe's inner anger or anxiety showed; instead he arranged his features into a careful mask of petulant disappointment. "So early! Well, I did tell him I would be here at one. He was so set on starting today! Have you any idea of where he went?"

"No, sur. Didn't he tell you?"

Ludlowe saw the suspicion flare quickly in the landlord's eyes and gave a frivolous little laugh. "Lord, no. I wasn't to go with him, only to deliver some papers. . . ." His voice dropped to a hoarse whisper. "I wouldn't dream of telling just anyone this, but we're about to do a business deal that will. . . . Things have turned out better than we thought. And since he was in such a hurry, he doesn't know about it. Serves him right for rushing off, doesn't it?"

The landlord nodded, seeing the Bell as a center of finance, frequented by men of money and power, a rival to Boodle's or White's. "It does seem a pity that Mr. Pascoe shan't know of his good fortune."

"Yes, but he was so set on getting away. I can get the news to him at his home in a few days. Serve him right if he has to come straight back. Pity he wasn't going directly home; I could overtake him on the road then," Ludlowe said diffidently, watching from the tail of his eye the struggles passing over the landlord's face.

"Sur, I wouldn't normally say anything, but seeing as ye be such a great friend of Mr. Pascoe's and have such wonderful news fer him, I might be able to help ye. The Bell is a friendly place, sur, and we take right good care of our patrons."

215

"I say, that is decent of you. Did he mention his route?"

"No, sur, nothing like that. It's just that I heard him asking the stableman about the inns on the Heath. . . . Sounded like he was heading through Hampstead."

Ludlowe knew the area; desolate, frequented by footpads and highwaymen, with a scattering of hedge taverns. Yes, Seth would choose such a place, just as he had chosen this one, hiding among the hunted and using their fears as his protection. Who would have thought the lad to have so much cunning?

"Hampstead. That's a big area. Did he mention a place?"

"No, sur, but the stableman recommended the Owl and Bush as being a respectable place. Though it isn't a patch on the Bell, sur. Will ye be wanting another drink, sur?"

"No, I think not. I must catch Mr. Pascoe. I'll be sure to tell him of your kindness," Ludlowe said, nodding, throwing a sizable coin on the bar. There was no time to lose and he wanted to be well away from the Bell before the mood of the place got any uglier. Besides, poor Mickleham must be nigh frozen and they still had a long way to go.

"Thank ye, sur, thank ye! It was a pleasure serving ye. Don't forget to tell yer friends about the Bell!" Eli Latham pocketed the coin with a grin of pleasure and spent the rest of the night in a hazy dream of success and power as the landlord of the highly popular social spot, the Bell Tavern.

Phillipa came back to consciousness slowly, exploring the returning faculties carefully, for everything was overlaid with a fiery red glaze of pain which finally localized into a great throbbing knot on the side of her head. At least she was still now, having hazy recollections of being in movement, a pitching and lurching that had done dire things to her stomach, and of being bundled in a great amount of cloth, where somehow the cold penetrated but breathable air did not. She was cold now.

Cautiously she opened her eyes, at first checking to see if she were alone before taking in the appearance of her surroundings. It was a most unprepossessing chamber. The ceiling was low and in the grudging light of the single candle, stained plaster showed between the dark beams. Mismatched and ugly, the heavy furnishings took on monstrous proportions in the poor light. A niggardly fire smoldered in the grate, sending forth little light and less heat.

Her head was clearing; it was still painful and doubtless would be that way for several more days at least, but the worst was over. It was not much warmer by the fire, but it was better than lying on the bed, which had smelled most suspiciously of damp and was probably verminous.

Pulling a small stool closer to the hearth, Phillipa tried to examine her situation. She had received Geraint's note, stepped outside the garden gate . . . and waked up here with an outrageous thirst and a broken head.

Why would Geraint do such a thing to her? To ruin her? There was a much easier way to do that, merely spread around the tale of her stay at St. Gregory's. Once the Duchess of Connaught and Mrs. Valelyn got hold of such a choice tidbit, her shaky reputation was ruined forever! She might as well emigrate or join a convent.

What could he possibly have planned for her? She dug in her pocket, smoothed the crumpled note, then moved closer to the candle, trying to read the faint smudges of pencil. *I must see you. About St. Gregory's. The back garden gate in one hour.*

Frowning, Phillipa read the note again and again, as if sheer repetition would reveal more information. Why had she been so sure that this had come from Geraint? She had never seen his handwriting, but somehow, examined logically, this ill-formed scrawl and choppy phrasing didn't seem to belong to Geraint at all. He could be terse, how well she knew, but somehow even his terseness had more style than this.

Phillipa rubbed her chilly arms and stared into the pathetic fire. She had done it again. Stupid, foolhardy creature that she was, she had stepped headfirst into another imbroglio, and Heaven only knew how she was going to emerge unscathed from this one. Would she never learn to think first?

It was the mention of St. Gregory's that had done it; after all, besides Geraint, who knew of her escapade there? Who would know that she had more than a passing interest in the school, that the mention of it would bring her running? Mamma, Papa, Aunt Beatrice, Ronnie, Letty . . . none of them could be behind this; she might as well suspect herself. That only left Sir Percy Hightower—ridiculous!—Geraint, and . . .

"Good evening," Seth said.

Absurdly Phillipa's first thought was that he had changed during the past months. Soberly dressed and neatly groomed, Seth appeared a completely different creature. Had she not seen the expression in his eyes, her identification might not have been as certain so quickly.

He closed the door behind him as quietly as he had opened it, but made no move toward her. "I am glad to see that you waked."

Phillipa stood quietly. "Don't you dare come near me."

"I don't intend to . . . now. Don't you know that if I were going to make such advances, I could have done so while you were unconscious? Desirable as your body may be, I am out for other game at the moment. Don't give up though; who knows what might work out?"

"Get out of here!"

He made a credible bow, just the sort one would have expected from an aspirant cit. "As you wish, miss. Just remember . . . you can't get out of here. The door is locked, and the servants are in my pay."

"What do you want? Why did you bring me here?"

"You are a very valuable property, miss. It will be interesting to see—"

"What do you mean?" Phillipa all but screamed, her control breaking, but Seth's only answer was a slight, frightening smile and the sound of the door closing behind him.

Shaken by a chill that the biggest fire in England would not abate, Phillipa sank back onto the stool, huddling her cloak around her. In all her wildest imaginings she had never thought that Seth would actually come after her and that she in a moment of idiocy would put herself in his power. For a number of minutes she sat huddled like that, stunned and waiting for she knew not what.

Still, for all that she was a female, the blood of sturdy English warriors flowed in Phillipa's veins, and the courage that had taken her through the horror of St. Gregory's would not be long kept down. Phillipa squared her shoulders with a gesture that would not have disgraced a fighting man and tried the door; Seth had told the truth, for it was locked. A quick glance around the room showed no hope of a weapon strong enough to disturb such a sturdy portal of aged oak. That left only the window.

This place had been built sometime during the reign of Elizabeth and the windows were small and leaded in the height of that fashion. Apparently, Phillipa thought, they had not been opened since that time, either. The hasp was old yet sturdy and only after supreme effort did it yield, swinging open to disclose a disappointingly small aperture. Disregarding the chill rain that peppered her skin, Phillipa leaned out, only to pull her head back in quickly, her senses swimming. From the tiny window there was a sheer drop to the ground of a good three stories. *This room must be in the attic!* Phillipa thought with dismay. It would be madness to attempt such a drop. Not only were there bushes below, but she could not see the ground and there was not a tree anywhere within reach. It would surely mean a broken leg or worse if she were to attempt such a jump.

Her mind now working at full speed, Phillipa took but a second to curse the weakness that had left her stuporous, wasting precious seconds. Time was important; unless she possessed herself of the magical powers of the Irish leprechauns and flew up the chimney, there were only two methods of escape from the room—the door and the window. The door was locked and unbreakable; that left only the window.

Holding tightly to the sill, once again Phillipa leaned out into the darkness. The faint glow of lamplight from the stables opposite gave scant illumination to her inspections. This room was high up on the back side of the house; doubtless Seth had chosen it for that very reason, knowing that it would make a very secure prison.

Below and a little to the left was a roof, probably to the kitchen or sculleries, just a story high and added on to the original structure. If she could only get onto that roof . . . Phillipa's heart and mind began to race and she leaned even further out. Yes, the outside was half timbered, just as she had thought. The beams were huge, as befitted such a house, but the wattle and daub was beginning to erode, leaving a shelf slightly wider that her hand. If she could get outside and inch along that shelf until she could drop onto the lower roof . . . the whole distance she would have to traverse couldn't be more than six feet. Still—here she couldn't resist a self-pitying look downward three stories to the dark bushes—that would mean six feet of clinging to the side of a building like a fly, hoping for handholds and risking certain injury and possible death if she should fall. But, she thought, Seth awaited her if she stayed.

Only the clumsy handling of the lock warned her that the door was going to open. She had no time to close the window before Geraint was there in the center of the room, holding out his arms to her. Phillipa flew into them as if it were the most natural thing in the world, not stopping to think or even berate her treacherous heart. For the moment all she could think of was the feel of his strong arms around her, his muscular shoulder under her cheek, the feel of his lips traveling down from her hair to her lips, which were waiting eagerly. . . .

"Phillipa . . . dearest girl . . . did he hurt you? Are you all right?"

"I'm not hurt . . . my head is sore, that's all."

His gentle fingers probed the tight knot over her ear and he swore. "The swine! I came as soon as I could, as soon as I got the note."

"Note?"

"He thinks I have the money from that business at the school. He wanted what he thought was his share of it. I'm sorry it took me so long, but I had to find out where he was going. Oh, Phillipa, my darling, my dearest . . ." Once more his lips found hers, wild and possessive, his body against hers until they were as one being, darkly silhouetted by the dying fire.

Phillipa clutched at him, willing her mind to believe and finally not caring for anything but the feeling of his lips and his arms and the nearness of him. She molded against him, feeling the chill of his soaked clothing and the strength of his muscles, wanting to feel nothing but the nearness of him for the rest of her days, her mind finally capitulating to what her heart had known for months.

"Geraint . . . my darling, don't ever let me go. I can't fight any more. I love you."

222

Ludlowe drew a ragged breath and looked down at her face—so open, so trusting—looking up at him with an expression of love that could melt the hardest resolve. "I've waited so long to hear you say that, you don't know . . . But you're shivering. What were you doing leaning out that window?" Reluctantly he released her to close the sash, then turned back, his face blanched. "My God! You weren't thinking . . . ?"

All Phillipa could think at the moment was how handsome he was, his face etched by the firelight, his damp hair like a shining helmet, his look of concern as he embraced her again. "I thought Seth was coming," she said simply.

Only the involuntary tightening of his muscles showed the depth of his emotion. "Seth will never bother you again, my dearest. I will see to that. No matter what has happened, we'll solve it some way. I won't let you out of my life again. I love you."

Phillipa gave a tiny sob. "I've dreamed so often of you saying that. I never thought it could happen. I thought you and Seth—"

"We don't have much time, my love." He kissed her once more, thoroughly, and then led her to the fire. "You're freezing. Now, we must think quickly. My friend is downstairs with Seth now, making sure that he doesn't disappear again. We sent a postboy to fetch Sir Percy Hightower, since he was the magistrate who originally handled the case. He can be persuaded that Seth is the only one left from Saint Gregory's, and I think I can convince Seth not to mention your name. . . ." His smile was ugly. "But we must make sure that Sir Percy doesn't see you!"

Growing cold from the inside out, Phillipa stood

just a little straighter, her composure hardening and her heart cracking.

"It will be easier all around if you appear to have nothing to do with this mess. I'm sure the servants and the innkeeper can be bought; the less they have to do with magistrates, the happier they'll be, I'm sure. There's no reason for anyone to know that you were mixed up in that mess at the school. . . . No one must ever suspect. I think it's best if you stay here until all the unpleasantness is over. Then I will come back . . . Oh, Phillipa, Phillipa. . . ." His hand brushed her cheek. "I tried so hard to hate you, but I can't. I give up. Will you be mine? I know this is the wrong time, but after almost losing you . . ."

"You mean . . . marry you?" Phillipa asked in a very small voice. It was so tempting, so tempting, but in some small recess of her mind was a memory of hate-filled eyes and a voice saying *"I will see you in Hell . . ."* when he thought her holding Ronnie in her clutches. Doubtless if he were sacrificing himself to save a friend, Geraint would be more than able to devise a very fitting version of Hell, and then it would be too late for the both of them. And, Phillipa thought, it would be a protection for him, as wives were unable to give evidence against their husbands. "And the past?"

He groaned as a man with a pain past bearing. "We will forget it."

"You no longer think me guilty?"

He frowned, pained. "There is no longer any reason to think of the past. We have the future. Isn't that enough?"

With a mouth of ashes, Phillipa said distinctly, "Not for me."

He turned, stony-faced, at the door. "We will discuss this later. No matter what happens, I will protect you from this unpleasantness. When Sir Percy is gone I'll come back for you. We have much to say to each other, Phillipa."

The sound of the lock turning was like a curse. He did not want her to see Sir Percy because he was afraid that she would give evidence against him; there was no other explanation. With a dead heart that refused to quit beating, Phillipa turned to the window.

Later she remembered that the traversing of the beam was not as frightening as it had promised to be, though whether this was from an actual physical ease or a complete numbness of her senses she never knew. Once she was over the kitchen roof, it became merely an athletic exercise, for it was a simple thing, though rather hard on the clothing, to slither down the sloping roof and drop from there to the ground.

The rain still fell, but she knew that it was imperative to put as much distance between herself and this place as possible. If she could get to the Grange—oh, if she could ever get to the haven of the Grange again, she would never leave it, not even for a day—or to London and Ronnie. Be Geraint a friend or not, Ronnie would protect her from him.

She rubbed her eyes. Surely she was tired, or her head wound was more serious than she had thought, for her yearning for Ronnie had made the man crossing the courtyard from the stables appear to be Ronnie for a moment. Was she going mad? But surely . . .

"Ronnie?"

There was enough light from the stable to guide astonished arms and to assure bewildered eyes. "Pia! By all that's holy! What are you doing here? You have a headache."

Hysteria bubbled up, a queer mixture of laughter and sobs, threatening to shake her drenched body apart, until a smartly applied slap defeated her completely and she fell weeping on her cousin's bosom. "Oh, Ronnie! Of course my head aches. I've been hit and imprisoned and . . . please take me home, Ronnie. I don't know how you found me, but I'm so glad you did."

"Found you? Good God, Pia, what happened to the side of your head? That's a veritable goose egg!"

"Take me home, Ronnie."

"All right. Let's take you inside and I'll make arrangements—"

"No!" Phillipa clutched at her cousin, fear widening and darkening her eyes. "He's still in there. No one must know, Ronnie. Please!"

"All right. Stand here. I've got to take leave of someone, but I'll be right back."

"Ronnie—" Pia choked and then began to cry again.

CHAPTER TWENTY-SIX

The next hours were just about the worst Lord Ronald had ever known in his life, including his wilder experiences in the Peninsula. Later he would look back in absolute amazement at his idiotic blindness, but at the moment his brain was too full of disparate images for him to even try to make any connection between them. Pia, appearing out of the dark, drenched and uncharacteristically hysterical; a harmless enough looking young cit alone in the sole private parlor, who pulled a wicked-looking knife; Pablo, with a face as dark as thunder, having to be physically restrained from beating the young man to a senseless pulp . . . Ronnie's plate was full enough just trying to keep everyone pacified. Pia wept and clung, behaving as he had never before seen her. Although he knew his duty was to take her home immediately, she would not let him move until she had extracted his promise not to tell anyone of her presence nor to make a stir about his going.

Ronnie frowned, as he was destined to do a lot that night. He had left Pia hiding in the stable, wrapped in the doubtful warmth of his sodden cloak, weeping as

227

if her heart would burst. Now he was thinking furiously as he crossed the courtyard, trying to find a way to take leave of Ludlowe without seeming so odd or uncaring that his suspicions would be aroused. Not that Pia had anything to fear from Ludlowe, but he had given his word. . . .

All in all it went rather better than he could have hoped. After Ludlowe was assured that the postboy had been sent immediately on his errand to London, he seemed almost glad to see Ronnie go, and the younger man's rather limp tale of a forthcoming attack of ague passed without undue attention. The cit lay sprawled on the floor like a dead man and Ludlowe, wearing an expression Ronnie had never seen even after the worst of the Peninsular action, stalked the room as if only waiting for another opportunity to mill him down again. Had Pia not been waiting, Ronnie would have been eager to stay to see how he could best help his friend—and to satisfy his own curiosity about Ludlowe's erratic behavior tonight—but perhaps if he could get Pia to talk, some of the mysteries would be solved.

There was ample time to talk, for once away from the tavern, the couple's progress was slow, hampered not only by dark and rain, but by a tired horse. Mickleham had decided against hiring a vehicle or another horse at the inn, fearing discovery and the ensuing inquiry. There would be another inn along the way where, with the aid of a plausible story and a bit of blunt, he would be able to procure something suitable. At this pace, however, it seemed that the next inn was some distance away and with the cold rain pouring over him, Pia a dead weight in his arms, and the night as black as the inside of a cow's stomach, Ronnie began to question his wisdom.

Pia sighed, breaking the long silence that had begun to lead her cousin into thinking her either dead or unconscious. It was a welcome sound, for the silence had been even more out of character and harder to bear than the weeping hysterics.

"All right, Pia?" Ronnie hugged her briefly and was rewarded by a gentle pat on his arm.

"Yes. It's so dark. How can you see where we're going?"

Ronnie smiled slightly. This was more like the old Pia. "I can't. I'm trusting Apollo to take us."

"Good Apollo. I hope he isn't too tired, carrying the both of us. How did you find me, Ronnie? How did you ever find me?"

"Just lucky," he answered with utter truthfulness. "Don't you think you owe me an explanation?"

"Ronnie . . . Oh, Ronnie, I can't! It's just so horrible . . ."

"Pia . . . sooner or later you're going to have to tell someone; hadn't it better be me so that between us we can work out something to tell everyone else?"

"You're right, of course, Ronnie," she said after a moment, her voice curiously small. "It will be such a weight removed from me . . . such a relief . . ."

Almost bursting with curiosity, Ronnie waited until she spoke again, some moments later. Some inner wisdom counseled him to remain silent, for any speech at all would distract her. Whatever she was going to say didn't concern only tonight's escapade, but had its roots who knew how far in the past.

"At the inn tonight . . . did you see a tall man with

dark hair? He had on a dark-blue riding coat . . .
Oh, Ronnie, how can this be happening? He's a rogue
and a murderer and Heaven only knows what else and I
love him! I've loved him for months and months, and
then when I found out what a rogue he was I couldn't
stop loving him!" Phillipa began to cry again, little
soft hiccupping sobs that blended with the worsening
rain.

It had never been said by anyone that Lord Mickleham was overburdened in the brain-box, but suddenly
with a blaze of intellect as bright as any lightning
bolt, he saw the entire situation. "Your schoolmaster!
That fellow is your schoolmaster!" Even as Pia murmured her affirmative, Ronnie was putting pieces in
place and the resultant crazy-quilt design actually
made sense—as well as solving a few questions. Ludlowe had been in England while Phillipa had been
pulling her stunts. . . . Despite the wound, he had
gone home because his younger brother had died! In
the light of present disclosures, it would not be too
farfetched to assume that he too had attended St. Gregory's and that because of his brother's death, Ludlowe had acted in mirror fashion to Pia, assuming a
menial role to gain entrance to the school in order to
catch the miscreants. Then, Pia had fallen in love with
the schoolmaster, only to believe him a rogue when he
turned up in London with a fortune. She had still
been in the schoolroom, as he himself had been when
Ludlowe was last on the Town. And . . . could it be
that Ludlowe had fallen in love with Pia, too? That
would explain his moodiness of the past few weeks,
his sarcastic remarks about love and women. And,
Ronnie thought with no little dismay, to make the tan-

gle complete, Ludlowe probably thought Phillipa to be a villainess. It would have been uproariously funny had it not been so close and involving people about whom he cared deeply.

Pia was talking again, haltingly, painfully, telling of her love for this man who called himself Geraint Catton, of meeting him in London, of the receipt of the note that she assumed came from him, of her abduction . . .

"That's what I want to know. Who did take you off? I know . . . I mean, I'm assuming, it wasn't this Catton fellow."

"Did you see a young man there? Blondish hair, brown suit? That was Seth. He sent the note."

The young cit! thought Ronnie; he had been wondering where that young man fit in, and now Ludlowe's violent actions made sense. For a moment he wished to be back at the tavern again; it would be greatly satisfying to get in a few licks at that young scoundrel himself.

"So when Seth locked me in I thought I was lost . . . I was looking for a way of escape when Geraint came in. I'm ashamed, Ronnie, but even then I still loved him . . . and I told him so. How could I be so contemptuous of Arnold's memory that I could feel so shameless about one of his murderers? He bade me wait and locked me in . . . Sir Percy had been sent for and he didn't want me talking to him. Said he wanted to protect me! He even offered me marriage, Ronnie, he even said he loved me. How convenient that a wife can't give evidence against her husband!"

That would have been during Ludlowe's quick trip upstairs, while he had been left to guard the unconscious cit, Ronnie decided, for just before that he had been commissioned to send the reluctant postboy to London with an urgent message. No wonder Ludlowe had been so secretive about the errand and about his time upstairs; he had been protecting Pia from discovery . . . but why should he protect her from her own cousin and why should Pia . . . ? Of course; it was the final proof. Neither one of them knew who the other really was. What a tangle!

"Then when he left I knew I couldn't stay there, so I climbed out the window and down onto the shed and found you. Oh, Ronnie, Ronnie, what am I going to do?"

Ronnie looked out into the dark and made a vow. "Trust me, Pia. I'll take care of you."

"Are you going to marry Letty?" she asked much later.

"There doesn't seem to be much hope of that. M'mother doesn't seem to care overmuch for the match, and the Duchess of Connaught seems to have taken an extreme dislike to you and anyone connected with you."

"Cowheart."

"That was uncalled for, Pia."

"No, it wasn't. If you love Letty—and I know she loves you dreadfully—do something about it. Post down to Coombs Farm and talk to the duke. He's fond of her, and if you want to marry her, get his permission. As for your mother . . . well, I'll wager your father would never have let her lay the law down to him and she thought him the best of men. Lud, Ronnie, you're a man! Act like one!"

After that Ronnie said nothing, but Phillipa could

practically hear him thinking. *Well*, she thought, *let him think!* The idea should have occurred to him long ago. At least if he ended up marrying Letty there would be some good out of this whole mess. Maybe they would let her come and stay with their children and play aunt, since her own future seemed so bleakly devoid of any hope of domestic happiness.

It was almost dawn when they finally arrived at the Grange, after a night of unremitting rain, several missed turnings, and an indifferent carriage coaxed from a reluctant innkeeper. Lord Ronald accepted his aunt and uncle's thanks for protecting Phillipa and bringing her home, but declined their hospitality beyond that of breakfast while his clothing was being dried as best as possible and the loan of a fast horse. There was much to do, and it had to be done in London. His mother must be out of her mind with worry, and the better it would be for all concerned when the ton was officially notified that Miss Stanhope-Fredericks had left Town suddenly to go the bedside of her ailing mother as a dutiful daughter should.

CHAPTER TWENTY-SEVEN

Phillipa sat in the little parlor, staring abstractedly into space, Mrs. Cutterworth's latest novel—which Miss Bunch had sworn to be so delicious and so terrifying that it would be impossible to put down—lying on her lap, open to the same page she had read at least ten times. When Miss Bunch had heard of Miss Stanhope-Fredericks's return to the Grange the previous week as an aid and comfort to her mother, she had loudly lauded such filial duty and squelched with difficulty a most bitter jealousy. To leave London . . . ! Still, as a Christian and the well-taught daughter of a man of God, Miss Bunch stifled her uncharitable feelings and promptly appeared at the Grange with the commendable intention of seeing that Miss Stanhope-Fredericks did not fall into a fit of the dismals after leaving the gaieties of London. To ensure that Miss Stanhope-Fredericks should appreciate her gestures of friendship, Miss Bunch brought along a generous supply of novels, lovingly hand chosen from among her own favorites, all rather startlingly unsuitable for a vicar's daughter.

Although her dedicated benefactress had been duly thanked, Phillipa had decided, after glancing over a few volumes, that they were as dull as their donor, whom she had never really liked, for all that they had grown up in close proximity. Each book was distressingly like all the others, being mainly concerned with the social and amorous intrigues of High Society, and having been written both by and for those to whom the doors of the ton would never be opened. Every character had a title and it was My Lord this and Your Grace that until it became ludicrous, and it seemed that there was not one plain Miss, Mrs., or Mr. in London. Several times Phillipa had thought it a pity she was not gifted in the way of a novelist, where she could write the story of her own adventures. But if she controlled the story, she would guarantee a happier ending.

Fanchon interrupted her reverie, which had drifted away from books, either reading or writing them, to taller, darker subjects. Phillipa, more conscious of her mother's fragile health since her return home, inquired if she were needed. During her stay she had become a companion to her mother, reading to her and disentangling her crochet work. Mr. Stanhope-Fredericks swore heartily that Phillipa was leading her mother back to complete health. Because of her fragility, Mrs. Stanhope-Fredericks had been told only a little of the story behind Phillipa's bedraggled dawn appearance, and Mr. Stanhope-Fredericks felt sure there was something more than his daughter was telling him, though the idea of her being kidnapped by that villain from St. Gregory's was quite bad enough.

Aware of Miss Phillipa's self-imposed duties, Fanchon hastened to assure her that her mother had not rung, rather that her cousin Lord Mickleham was here to see her. Having received the curiously impatient order to admit him at once, he went away smiling inwardly with satisfaction as one only can when one has known both young people since they were in shortcoats.

"Pia?"

"Ronnie!" Phillipa flung herself into her cousin's outstretched arms, the novel flying to the floor with a disrespect that would have sent Miss Bunch into a spasm, for to be sure the story of the attempted seduction of Lady Constantina by Everard, Earl of Valdo, and her timely rescue by her true love, Captain Lord Bartholomew Trewithag of the Hussars, was one of her favorites.

"How goes it, Pia? You looked properly bluedeviled when I came in."

Hand in hand, they settled in the tiny window seat, barely warmed by the pale winter sunshine, the unhappy book forgotten.

"Oh, Ronnie, I was. I have been slowly going mad down here with no news and no way to find out anything without ruining everything! Tell me what happened."

With seeming unconcern Ronnie inspected one of the handsome gold buttons that adorned the front of his regimentals and frowned. This part was the trickiest going, and somehow the plan that had appeared so simple on his ride back to London last week now seemed to loom impossibly overwhelming.

"Damned—sorry—accursed thing's coming off. Must speak to Peters about that." Then, just as his shortpatienced cousin was coming close to committing a most unladylike violence, Ronnie said, "Nothing.

Nothing at all happened. Hightower was able to apprehend that Seth fellow in good fashion and he'll stay locked away for a good time because of that business at Saint Gregory's. I had a little talk with Sir Percy—I didn't remember that he was your godfather—and he agreed with me that there was no need to mention this last affair."

"Thank you for that. And the other?" Phillipa's voice was very soft, her eyes riveted to the button whose security Ronnie was so brutally testing.

"Other? There was no other, not that we could find." The button flew free. "Look at that! There's just no workmanship anymore. I shall have to have Peters check every single button on all my coats, for it would be the very Devil—sorry—to replace one."

"Thank you, Ronnie." For an exquisite moment Phillipa's eyes filled with tears and her cousin was sorely tempted to blow the game and tell her all, but he held his tongue and the moment passed.

"Oh, just look . . ." Phillipa flew to the fallen volume and tried to put it aright. "Oh, dear . . . the cover is bent and there's a page torn . . ."

"What is that? Here, let me see. *Constantina's Choice; or, The Quest of True Love Fulfilled.* Good God, what are you doing with this? Are you actually reading such trash?"

"But of course. After all, dear Miss Bunch did pick out her very favorites to bide me company while I was at home. She said that as they were all about the London scene, I should feel less lonely reading them. Miss Bunch said that she found *Constantina's Choice* a most edifying and morally uplifting book, and so incredibly romantic that she almost suffered a spasm the first time she read it."

"Miss Bunch? Bunch . . . she one of the parson's brood? Probably the one with a face like a rabbit," Ronnie mused and Phillipa made some comment about the lady's teeth being unfortunate, but that she did adore a good romantic novel.

"And she told me the whole story . . . almost acted it out and probably would have, had there been anyone around into whose arms she could have sunk. She had even memorized the speeches he said to her— Captain Lord Whatever-his-name-is to Constantina— and she said them all to me—"

Ronnie recoiled. "Well, don't you go saying them to me or I shall have a fit of the vapors myself!"

"Don't worry. I couldn't if I tried, not without giggling at least. Would you like me to sew your button back on before you lose it?"

As if studying the matter, Ronnie weighed the button in his palm, turning it over and over with his fingers. It was a momentous decision, to play with people's lives, people he loved, and for all his derring-do Ronnie was not a momentous man. War was simple: one obeyed one's superiors, tried to act as a gentleman, and killed the enemy. Playing deus ex machina was more fraught with danger than he would have supposed. It was all very well to make mischievous plans that could have come straight out of one of those lurid romances, but when people's lives and happiness were at stake, the chance of a mistake loomed large.

"So serious over a button, Ronnie?"

"Huh? No, not the button, not at all . . . damned

silly things, buttons. Always coming off. I need your help, Pia."

"Of course, Ronnie. What?"

"Well, I'm going to marry Letty."

At least some good was coming out of this mess, Phillipa thought. She truly loved Letty and now felt good that her friend would have a happy life. "That's wonderful! But how can I help you?"

"I'm coming to that. We talked it over and decided against a big church wedding. Letty won't say anything, but I think she's afraid her mother will upset it in some way. I am too, if you want to know the truth. Damned vindictive woman, that. And, it just wouldn't be proper for the bride to be married out of the groom's house, so we decided to see if she could be married from the Grange, with your mother and father as sponsors."

"Ronnie, that's a perfectly splendid idea! But what will the duke say?"

"He's agreeable. Seems he knows his wife better than anyone else. He said he'd come and of course stand the nonsense for anything Letty wants to spend."

"Poor man," Phillipa sighed. "And poor Letty. What a pity two such nice people have to work around such a creature as that Eustacia! But how marvelous that Letty should want to be married from here. I'm sure it will be all right, but we do need to get Mother's final approval. It will do her good to have something to think about besides the past. Let's go and ask."

Ronnie's smile was sheepish. "That's where m'mother and Letty are at the moment."

"They're here? Now? And you didn't tell me?"

"No . . . remember, I need your help, Pia. I wanted a chance to talk with you first."

"All right. I'll help you any way I can."

Ronnie took a deep breath. "You remember I wrote you about my friend Ludlowe? We were in Spain together. He's a good fellow—saved my skin a few times. Well, he's to be the best man. He's not been back in the country long—just a little longer than I—hasn't got many friends. The truth of the matter is, I'd told him so much about you that he's quite fascinated, and when the announcement party is held here . . . if your mother approves, of course . . . I'd be very obliged if you'd sort of look after him. He's heard so much about you, you see. . . ." He was stumbling, making a mull of it. Damn it all, why couldn't a man talk properly when he needed to?

Phillipa had gone pale. "Ronnie, I couldn't . . ."

"Well, curse it, Pia, I don't know what to do. Ludlowe's a nice enough chap, easy-going, but it would seem deuced odd—no, downright ramshackle—if after puffing you off to him for months I suddenly tell him you aren't receiving, and at my announcement party too!"

Phillipa then said with some asperity that announcement party or not, no one had asked him to "puff her off" to anyone, to which Ronnie replied that, like any self-respecting male relative, he felt responsible for her happiness and desired nothing more than to introduce her to an agreeable companion. "Besides," he added, as if it clinched the matter, "Ludlowe's a capital chap. You'll like him."

"I don't think I'll ever like anyone ever again," Pia said with unimaginable bleakness.

240

After a long pause in which he saw himself both saving and ruining Pia's happiness, Ronnie said, "I'm asking for your help, Pia. I know it's an imposition, especially after what you've just been through, but I need your assistance. I'd hoped not to have to bring it up, but I do think you owe me something—"

"Of course, Ronnie!" Phillipa cried, awash in remorse. "What an ungrateful wretch I am, and I do owe you so much. What can we do?"

It was some thirty minutes later when Phillipa, chock-full of stories illustrating Ludlowe's heroism and gallantry and instructions on making him feel wanted and welcome at the Grange, was finally free to join the female contingent of the bridal party and to hide her own misery amid the joy of her loved ones.

CHAPTER TWENTY-EIGHT

Lord Ronald Mickleham felt uncommonly pleased with himself; a glance out the window showed that the sun was already high. No matter; he had put out considerable effort this past week and had arrived at the Grange well past dark the night before. Tonight was the official party announcing his betrothal to Letty—ah, Letty! Was there ever a sweeter, more angelic, more wonderful woman in the world? And, if that weren't enough to complete his fill of happiness, tonight he would also straighten out the muddle between Paul and Phillipa. It was still a mystery how they had gotten things so tangled between them, but that was past now, thanks to his unstinting efforts.

Ronnie drank his chocolate leisurely and then dressed, choosing his clothes carefully. Today was the start of a new life and one did not choose attire for such auspicious occasions haphazardly. Tonight he would be formally betrothed to Letty and—if things went as he had planned—it just might be a double betrothal, if Ludlowe and Pia were as true in their feelings as they seemed to be.

It had taken the better part of a week to convince Ludlowe that he should come to the betrothal party—and later the wedding—as his best man. Listening to Ludlowe's talk with the added intelligence of Phillipa's information, Ronnie had been able to deduce just how far things had gotten mixed up. It was almost as good as a play.

Finally deciding to join the family, Ronnie found his mother and aunt in the morning room, chattering happily along on various mutual topics. After kissing them each on the cheek and accepting their congratulations on such a happy day, he leaned against the window embrasure. In a way he was happy that they had settled in this room, for from here he could see a good stretch of the road. Timing was now becoming important. Ludlowe had said that he would arrive no later than noon and Ronnie intended to be very sure that neither of his principals saw the other before he was ready. Since noon was not long off, Ronnie felt secure in watching for his friend. Once Ludlowe was in the park, Ronnie could find Pia and arrange a suitable introduction. He grinned.

"It would be foolish to ask if you are happy, Ronnie."

"I'm very happy, Aunt Arabella. Today is a wonderful day."

"Indeed it is," his mother replied, carefully setting a stitch. "It only proves that sometimes prayers are answered."

Ronnie smiled. "What prayers did you have, Mother? That Letty would not refuse me at the last minute?"

"That too, but I specifically had Phillipa in mind more than you or Letty."

From the window Ronnie could see a smart phaeton and set of matched chestnuts that could only belong to Paul Ludlowe, but he could not move. "Pia?"

Mrs. Stanhope-Fredericks looked up with a smile. "Do you think Letty would mind if tonight were made into a double betrothal party?"

Ronnie's mouth fell open. "A double betrothal? Pia?"

Beatrice calmly snipped at her thread, then paused to admire her handiwork. "Yes. It seems almost too good to credit, but Sir Rupert Longstreet called this morning to renew his suit."

"And Pia is with him now?" Ronnie asked in a queer, strangled voice.

"Yes. We've been expecting the outcome these last five minutes, but it always seems to take so long for that young man to actually get anything said—"

With the clean enunciation of an epithet more suited to a barracks than a ladies' salon, Lord Ronald

243

Mickleham flung himself into the corridor, leaving the two ladies staring after him in shock and wonder.

Sir Rupert held out his hand—an honorable, large, work-scarred hand. "I'm asking you again, Miss Stanhope-Fredericks . . . Phillipa . . . my dear . . . Will you do me the honor of becoming my wife?"

Phillipa looked dully at the outstretched hand. If she accepted it, she would have a very simple, ordered life, a nice house, and probably a number of children, and someday she would be a countess. It sounded like a very nice future, but how could she face every day of the rest of her life looking at someone who wasn't Geraint, living with someone who wasn't Geraint, bearing children who weren't Geraint's? With wide, frightened eyes she looked into Longstreet's face and knew the answer she must give.

"Pia! Here you are." Ronnie catapulted into the room without even so much as a knock, which was an odd thing, for usually his manners were of the most exquisite.

Longstreet's face flushed an angry red. What a time for an interruption! A few more moments . . . She had been just about to accept him, he knew, from the dazed and gentle expression on her face. Doubtless she had thought his ardor had cooled and his renewed suit had been a surprise.

"Miss Stanhope-Fredericks and I were just having a private conversation, Mickleham . . ."

Ronnie grinned idiotically. "Oh? So sorry to have interrupted it, but knew you wouldn't mind. You can pick up again later. Pia, can I borrow you a moment?"

Phillipa nodded dumbly and went to her cousin's

side, completely oblivious to her suitor's rising temper. Ronnie said something politely soothing and then hustled Phillipa down the hall, breathing a prayer of thanks that he had been in time. Why hadn't any of the ninnyhammers in this family told him sooner that Longstreet was still lurking about? How easily that could have caused a fatal error!

"Ronnie, what is it? You're acting like a lunatic."

"I have the right to act like a lunatic if I want. I'm the one getting married. Besides, you didn't really want to talk to that fusty old farmer, did you?"

Phillipa planted her feet firmly, bringing them to a dead stop in the center of the Blue Salon. It was a gloomy, dark chamber, usually used after funerals and eminently suitable for such depressing deeds. Taking a deep breath, Phillipa decided that the future must be faced now and that this was as good a time and place to do it as any. Besides, Longstreet might be her last chance.

"He asked me to marry him, Ronnie."

"Did you accept him?"

"You didn't give me a chance, bursting in like that!"

Ronnie's voice took on a somber note. "Do you want to marry him?"

"Yes. No. I don't know. . . . He's considered a good match . . ."

"Pia . . . do you love him?"

"How can you ask me that? You know . . ."

Ronnie grinned foolishly. "Well, that's no trouble then. I'm calling in your debt to me, Pia, and now."

"Now?"

"Now. Ludlowe's just arrived and . . ."

"Him? Now? Oh, Ronnie, I can't . . . Sir Rupert . . ."

245

"Pia, you promised! Knight's honor!"

The old fealty oath from childhood held, just as Ronnie had hoped it would. Phillipa nodded, then squared her shoulders like a good knight. "I suppose you want me to meet him now. Well, all right. Just give me a moment to collect myself."

"That's a good girl. I'll go on down, so he won't have to wait in the hall, but don't be long!" With a hasty and surprising buss to the cheek, Ronnie was gone.

The mirror in the Blue Salon was as depressing as the rest of the chamber, cloudy and marked by damp. Phillipa's reflection stared out at her, watery and distorted, much like her interior self at the moment, she thought as she started to smooth her hair back into place.

"Ronnie!" Only Letty's warning call saved Lord Mickleham from a direct physical collision with his betrothed. She hastily stepped back from his hurried path and reacted with highly satisfactory alarm as he twirled her around high off the floor. "Ronnie, have you lost your senses?"

"No, my dearest. I'm about to pull off the biggest strategic coup of my career! Come and watch the fun, but not a word." Tucking her arm through his, Lord Ronald Mickleham led a bewildered but unquestioning Lady Lettice Winterthorpe, at a sedate and dignified pace, into the entrance hall of Worthington Grange, just as Lord Paul Ludlowe relinquished his coat to an attentive Fanchon.

Ludlowe was impressed with the solid, unpretentious appearance of the Grange and remembered the affection with which Mickleham had spoken of his aunt, uncle, and cousin. It was reassuring to know that such families inhabited this island, and what a pity to think that it would soon be infiltrated by that crafty chit. Even after he had himself offered her marriage, she had preferred Mickleham, doubtless thinking—and correctly so—that he would be the easier to manage. It had taken a great deal of soul-searching before Ludlowe could agree to come here and wish the betrothed couple happy, but young Mickleham had been insistent and, as Ludlowe owed him his life for more than one occasion, it would have been unthinkable to deny.

Approaching matrimony seemed to agree with Lord Ronald, for his face was aglow and his step light, Ludlowe observed with a fine attempt at being dispassionate. That pretty, frail thing clinging to his arm must be the mysterious cousin Pia; strange, from Mickleham's talk, he would have thought her to be built along more generous lines. She looked familiar and it was a moment before Ludlowe could definitely place where they had met before. In the Park, and she had been walking with Phillipa . . .

"Ludlowe! You made good time down. How are you?"

"Fine, Mickleham. The roads are in top fettle—had to make only one change on the way down."

The two comrades exchanged a handshake. Letty's eyes widened with recognition and her all too ready tongue was stilled only by the insistent pressure of her beloved's hand on her arm.

"Aren't you going to introduce me, Ronnie?" Ludlowe asked with a fair counterfeit of his easy charm. "Or must I guess? This must be your cousin Pia of whom you've told me so much."

247

Ronnie's grin was obscene with suppressed triumph. "Sorry, old man. You've come wrong about. Letty, my dear, may I present Lord Paul Ludlowe, my dearest friend from the Peninsula? Paul, this is my bride-to-be, Lady Lettice Winterthorpe."

Paul Ludlowe was not a stupid man. The truth suddenly exploded in his brain with frightening impact, leaving him astonished and almost stuttering. "You mean . . . ?"

Phillipa's quick, light step sounded in the hallway; Ronnie had been waiting for that sound, almost bursting with pride at the way things were turning out. Not wishing to let anything go astray at this late date, he crossed the hall and, taking her arm in a strangely firm grip, he escorted her to the newcomer.

"Ronnie? Has your friend already arrived—?" Miss Stanhope-Fredericks's question trailed off to die in a strange strangled sound as a familiar form turned to face her.

"Pia, might I present Lord Ludlowe, of whom I've told you so much? Paul, my cousin Miss Phillipa Stanhope-Fredericks."

Had the earth itself opened at that moment and claimed her, Phillipa would have been grateful. The familiar hallway shimmered insubstantially and for a horrid moment the whole world began to whirl as if she would faint. How stupid she had been, so unpardonably dull not to see. . . . How could she bear such humiliation and the ridicule that would inevitably follow?

With an inarticulate cry Phillipa turned and fled the room, in her headlong flight giving her approaching parents and aunt a startling picture of her at a dead run, being pursued ruthlessly by a dark man with a grim face and a queer light in his eyes. On applying to Ronnie for an answer, he would say only that the game was not yet played out and they must wait for the final curtain. In fact, since this had been totally unplanned in his scenario—he had visualized them falling into a passionate embrace right there in the hall, under the beaming familial aegis—he was rightly allowing a little worry to creep into his mind, for neither his cousin nor his friend were noted for their stability of temper.

In the library Ludlowe finally ran her to earth, and that occured only because a footman scrimping his work had not oiled the catches to the French doors, causing them to stick. Realizing she was trapped, Phillipa turned to exhibit the same courage she had shown to Snodgress. She was defeated, perhaps, but dishonored, never! She looked up bravely, chin held high, and was irrationally infuriated to find him smiling.

"You might have told me!"

"I? You might have told me!"

"I thought you an unprincipled villain. My brother died at that place."

"So did mine, and I could let his death go unavenged no easier than you." He took a step closer. "Why did you run away that night at the inn? Do you realize I almost went mad when I realized the risks you took? And I didn't even know if you were safe or not . . ."

For some reason she was finding it very difficult to breathe. "I thought you were in league with Seth."

"And you thought I would hurt you?" Paul asked, his voice made harsh by angry incredulity.

"I didn't know! You certainly look as if you could now."

"I could very happily wring your neck now for all the misery you've caused me these past months. Oh, Phillipa . . . Maggie . . . Pia . . . whoever you are . . . whoever you might be . . . I love you. I offered for your hand when I thought you an unscrupulous adventuress. I'm offering for your hand now, and if you should turn out to be Queen of the Hottentots tomorrow, I'll offer for your hand then. I'll not give up until you accept me. I'll follow you wherever you go . . ."

Impulsive to the last, Phillipa held out her hand. "But I'm not going any—" She almost got the last word articulated before he crushed her in his arms, drowning her invitation in a very satisfying kiss.

To Ronald and his assembled gaggle of relatives, the silence from the back of the house was ominous. Some moments before, the contrapuntal slamming of doors had ceased and the ensuing quiet boded no good for anyone's nerves. This tension was not relieved by the sound of a single pair of footsteps approaching, nor by their proving to belong to Sir Rupert Longstreet. He was understandably upset, for it seemed that every time he came to offer for Miss Stanhope-Fredericks's hand, he was treated shabbily, a unique experience for a wealthy, unattached earl-to-be. If he were going to get back to Crowther Hall in time to be overseeing the drainage of the lower home farm field tomorrow, he should be leaving now, and he did not intend to leave without a firm answer.

Mickleham reacted with what Longstreet thought was unseemly levity, offering to track his cousin down, and Longstreet wondered if the man had the audacity to be foxed this early in the day on this day of all days. No one wished to be left out of the uncommon sport that was transpiring, so it was a full complement that Lord Mickleham led in search of the fugitive pair.

Eventually, in the ordered course of events, they came to the library, where Ronnie was especially gratified to see that not even the opening of the door and the collective gasps of six people could distract the couple from their amatory embrace. Longstreet was the first to demand an explanation.

"Well you see, old fellow, they've just become engaged," Ronnie said with proper pride.

"Engaged! But she said there was no one else! Is that Ludlowe!? Just how long has this been going on?"

Lord Mickleham, always courteous no matter the circumstances, politely replied with only a hint of a devilish grin, "His name is Paul Geraint Catton Ludlowe, and they've really only just met."

With no comment save a snort, Longstreet stalked from the house, leaving it and its lunatic inhabitants gladly. They were all a ramshackle bunch, with no idea of how to properly treat an earl-to-be. No one at all noticed his going.

Love—the way you want it!

Candlelight Romances

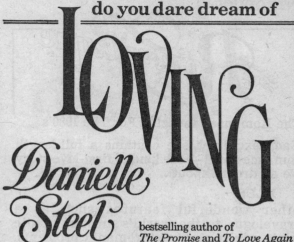

The first novel in the spectacular new
Heiress series

The English Heiress

Roberta Gellis

Leonie De Conyers—beautiful, aristocratic, she lived in the
shadow of the guillotine, stripped of everything she held
dear. Roger St. Eyre—an English nobleman, he set out to save
Leonie in a world gone mad.

They would be kidnapped, denounced and brutally separated. Driven by passion, they would escape France, return
to England, fulfill their glorious destiny and seize a lofty
dream.

A Dell Book   **$2.50 (12141-8)**